# A Trick of the Light

Emma Okell

*Emma Okell*

# A Trick of the Light

Published by
Arkett Publishing
A division of Arkettype
PO Box 36, Gaylordsville, CT 06755

Copyright © 2024 Emma Okell

All rights reserved under International and Pan-American Copyright
Conventions. No part of this book may be
reproduced or transmitted by any means without permission
in writing from the author.

ISBN 979-8348509729

Cover Artwork: Olivia Montoya

*A Trick of the Light*

*Dedicated to those who make their own hope.*

*Emma Okell*

# A Trick of the Light
by Emma Okell

## 1

I don't know how many times I squinted through the rocky crevice at that crack of light, faint by your standards and intoxicatingly brilliant by mine. There I was again, for the last time. Light this brilliant was as mesmerizing as music, even though it hurt my frail eyes. The thought of finally finding out what it was thrilled me and scared me at the same time.

Next to me, Iska also peered, fingers clasped on rocky rim to pull his face close. I could hear from the way his feet moved that he did not have to stand on his toes as I did.

"What do you think is in there?" Iska asked, not for the first time this week, this month, or this year.

"I don't know," I said.

But this time, he asked it differently, with more sincerity. And I answered differently, with more meaning.

"Obviously it's safe," I added. "Light doesn't burn where it isn't safe to breathe. I just wonder why the light burns even though they must know by now that it's safe."

"Unless it's like the surface," Iska said.

"That's different," I said. "That light is different. And it's not the light that's dangerous. It's everything else."

Iska hummed his agreement, and we silently stared.

"You'll come back," Iska asked, "right?"

"Yeah," I promised. "I will."

But as the old saying goes, promises easily spoken are easily broken. I didn't believe that saying. Now I know that you don't break promises because you want to break them. You break them because you didn't know at the time that they were impossible to keep.

I heard him move away from the crack, so I did too, looking at him. There were few places where we could see each other's faces. I didn't know at the time that even where there was enough light, I saw less than everyone else. Since my earliest memory of vision, I knew sight was warped, most of it blurry with patches of clarity. I turned my head so that Iska's face occupied the clearest patch of my sight.

"I can't convince you not to go," Iska said, "can I?"

"No," I said. "You can't. I promise, I'll go in, and I'll come right back out."

"No one's come back before," Iska said.

"I won't stay," I said.

More than a few people had gone there before me, all of them ambitious youths. None had returned. Some of us thought it was because that place full of light had brought them their wildest dreams. Most of us, really. But some of us had doubts. In my naivety, I did not.

"You promise? No matter how beautiful it is?"

"Yeah."

Iska was quiet a moment. Then he reached over, giving me a firm hug that reminded me that he was five days older than me.

"Good luck," he said.

"Thanks," I said. "I'll be quick."

Five minutes, I thought, and then I would hear my best friend's voice again.

I thought my plan was different from everyone else's, but in hindsight, we probably all did the exact same thing. I did not intend to go there to stay, only to see. I would go only just past the walls, not even fully in, so I could peer and eavesdrop. And then, I decided, I would go back to tell everyone what I'd seen and heard.

I looked over the wall. The wall was full of chips and cracks, but there were also larger holes. Some were too high up to reach, but some were down here. All I had to do was listen to the echoes of my footsteps to find one. A light tap, and you could feel as much as hear its faint whisper over the stony ground. And where the sound ended, you knew the floor gave way. But most caverns carried heavy echoes that gave me no doubt about where I was going. These were the sounds I used to reach the wall that surrounded the Light.

Sound guided me to my hiding place too. The places where the light leaked through were too high for me to reach and usually too small. I found only one that was low enough for me to reach, one where the Light shone through only faintly.

There were a few other places I tried. One was big enough for me to crouch into. It was a mere dip in the wall, though, and I heard its shallowness the moment I stepped in. The second place I had to stretch to reach, pulling myself up over a ledge with the strength of my spindly arms. It seemed promising at first. I crawled a short way through, far enough that I started to hear murmured voices, only to find that while it might extend into the depths of the Light, it was too small for me to fit my shoulders. I tsked in my frustration, and my small sound bounced back to me, revealing just how tiny the space was. I was surprised no one heard my complaint.

I almost did not find the third way in. It was behind a large stone that made the dip seem like it was part of the wall. But behind it, there was just enough room for a skinny teenager to crawl through.

It was not an easy crawl, and it made me nostalgic for the unexpected strength and flexibility of a small child. I wondered how such a small being could crawl and toddle without complaint when this amount of crawling already made my knees sore and my arms and legs complain. The rough stone did not help either. My hands and feet were calloused enough to bear them, but my arms and legs not so much.

But finally, I started to hear the voices again. A little farther, I started to hear a faint high-pitched buzzing sound, almost imperceptible, that grew a little louder with each handprint forward. And a little farther, I started to see a faint glow.

I moved as close as I dared. And I could see the Light.

The Light. It was nothing like any light I'd seen before, except maybe in the harshest daylight on the surface. It was brighter than anything I'd ever seen before, so bright that my unaccustomed eyes had to squint to shield it off.

I did not realize at the time that I had only seen the barest beginnings of the Light.

I vividly remember the scene. I could only see some of it. Most of it I heard. There was a platform, and there were people around it. I could only see three tall adults. I'm not sure if I could fully see them or if I just remember it that way now that I know there were three. Two men and one woman. Beside them, I thought I could faintly make out a small shadow, child-sized, or perhaps a larger person kneeling. And beside the platform, looking at the adults, if I squinted enough I could make out shapes that could have been a few more people. Already I could tell that this was a ceremony.

"The Light sustains us," one of the men was saying. "It guides us, provides for us, and shields us from the darkness of the world."

I pulled a little closer so I could hear better.

"But in return—"

The man stopped, looking toward me.

I felt my breath catch in my throat. I'd come too close, and he'd heard me, I thought.

And then I glanced. You have to understand that I did not understand at the time that light ignores edges and rims. So I was astonished to see that a small amount of light reached in, just enough to show the brown of my little finger against the beige of the stone. The Light suddenly seemed sentient to me, invading my hideaway. The Light had found me.

Keep in mind, I had no idea that if you can see light, then the light has already touched your face. If you can see, you can be seen.

The man stepped toward me. Too late I realized that I had only planned how to go in. The tunnel was too narrow for me to turn around, and I was too slow and clumsy to back into it.

The man took my arms and pulled me out. I was still too astonished to protest. How could he hear so well to know exactly where my arms were?

Now I was blinded. The light was so intense that it nearly left me paralyzed by its immense brightness.

"What were you doing hiding in that wretched darkness?" the man demanded.

I blinked, confused.

"Either you must want to corrupt our Light with darkness," the man said, "or you are fleeing the darkness to the Light. But we don't know which yet."

I gulped.

"The darkness is not all bad," I said.

I could tell from everyone's expressions that I had said the wrong thing.

"I mean, it can be," I said, thinking as fast as I could. "As you say, it's bad if it's trying to get rid of your Light. But darkness can be protective too. It can hide you so nothing hurts you. And that's what I was doing. I was hiding because I wanted to find out more about the light because it's really beautiful, but I didn't want to scare you. But I can go, and I won't bother you again."

I'd decided by then. No matter how great the Light might be, it was too much for me. This might be a promised land, but it had been promised to someone else.

The man looked at me, and he looked up. "Pelus."

I heard footsteps, but the person was close to me before I got a sense that he was a large man.

The first man pushed me into the large man's hand. "Bring him to retraining."

I didn't know what that was, but I knew already I didn't like it.

"Now, hold on," I said. "I can go, and you can seal up—"

"Take him away."

"Wait—" I protested.

But the man was already pulling me away.

"Open your eyes, boy," the man told me, not unkindly. "You'll fare better the sooner you get used to the light."

I tried to. I really did. But the light was so much I could scarcely squint. I kept my eyes closed.

I heard a squeak that stayed in place but a motion that swept so near to me that I flinched. I felt the draft of something over my face, created by a large plane far taller than me. The man pulled me past it.

"This will be your space for now," the man said. "Others will be here soon, but I need to go back for now."

He stepped away.

"Wait—" I started to say.

I heard the creak again and a thud.

The cavern was big. I could hear that much. My steps echoed only feebly to my sides and not at all to my front, although perhaps that was because that distant, ever-present buzzing swallowed my sound. The wall behind me echoed back in a strangely angular way. Disbelieving, I brought a hand to it, and I was startled by the flatness and the faint warmth. Walls were supposed to be rounded, lumpy, and cold. So, for that matter, were floors. I noticed now how flat and painful the floor was under my feet. Nothing for the arches of my feet to bite. Would it be harder to balance? And if I cracked my eyes open enough, I thought this cavern was a big span of white, but the brightness made it hard to tell. For a moment, I thought the whiteness flashed brighter.

I felt paralyzed. The floor was firm ahead of me, I could tell, but the room was so large with so little to mark it nearby. I could follow a wall, but how quickly would I become lost?

Even if I became lost, I could not put myself in a worse place than I already was.

I willed myself to explore the room, a hand upon the alien wall for a shred of comfort. I tapped the floor firmly with the ball of my foot, listening again for the echo, but I still heard only the flatness of the floor and the flatness of the wall, perfectly perpendicular to each other. What a chill that gave me.

I felt a crack in the wall and startled, feeling and listening. The crack was so fine that I could not hear it, thin as a hair. But I could hear something that projected out of the wall. Something round and hand-sized. But once again, this was alien. The roundness was symmetrical, and when I felt the object, it felt as perfect as it sounded. It was not solid to the wall, though. It rattled in my hand.

Perhaps, I thought, it could make this part of the wall move somehow. That would explain the moving plane. How it worked was beyond my guess, though. The round thing did not move outward or inward, nor did it turn, only rattled. Besides, I thought, I could not go out the way I went in. I would be caught.

I continued to step around.

When I walk, I test the ground with the balls of my feet. I can brush or tap the ground to hear, but I can also feel for sharp or lumpy edges before I step too heavily if I am in a strange place. What a strange place this was where my feet just about glided. As I stepped, though, I counted. Eight steps later, I could hear clearly hear the next wall in front of me, just as flat and just as perpendicular, not only to the floor but to this wall. I reached it, feeling the bizarre corner in fascination, and continued to walk.

Four steps later, I found another crack in the wall and another rattly sphere, and four steps later a second one. How fascinating, I thought. So many of these breaks in the wall. I would have to find out how the round things worked.

Eventually, I reached the first broken plane. The walls were each twenty four steps long. There were seven planes total: the one I had come through, two in the walls perpendicular to this wall, and one directly across from this one, and a tiny, thin one in the corner of the opposite wall from me. I had no idea if anything was in the center of this enormous cavern.

If I hadn't been alone, I would have explored the center. With two people, or more, you can quickly and safely make sense of the interior of a cavern. But on your own, the smallest danger could be deadly.

I don't know how long I was in that room. It felt so long. Endlessly long. I spent it staring, wondering, and pacing. I knew I was getting hungry. I had started to pace the wall yet again when I heard the first plane open.

"These will be your quarters for the next year," the big man's voice said. "The second door on the left is the boys' bedroom. The second one on the right is the girls' bedroom. You can settle yourselves in. Your teachers will be here to eat with you in a half hour."

"There's someone already here," a boy's voice said. It was changed but not mature, much like mine.

"He is part of your cohort," the man said.

I heard the plane close.

"He is?" a girl's voice asked. Something about her voice scared me, something in her undertone.

"Yes," the man said. "You may as well introduce yourselves to him."

I tried again to open my eyes. The light did not hurt so much now, but the world was still impossibly white. I could see a few people, but they were blurs because they were too far away. A few came closer to me. Most of them, I think. One stayed near the wall.

Then they came too close. Usually I wouldn't mind. Usually there is a comfort in feeling the body heat of a friend next to you or hearing their breath to remind you that they are there. But these were strangers, and I thought I heard a hostility in their breath. I told myself I only heard it that way because I did not know them yet.

I could see one boy's face clearly enough. He had tousled hair, bigger on top and shorter on the sides. I couldn't tell how much shorter it was on the sides, or how much longer on top, only that it didn't lay fully flat. I thought his nose was weirdly round.

I couldn't see the other boy as well. He was smaller-bodied. He was smaller than me.

And behind them a short way was another boy who frightened me most. He was very big, almost a whole head taller than me, and built like a boulder. I couldn't see his face except for his curly hair, but I was sure it was mean.

"You're from outside the city," the tousle-haired boy said.

"Yeah, I am," I said. "My name's Kimi."

The boy looked at the small-statured boy next to him. "By the living light. We're in luck!"

They clapped their hands together, laughing. I smiled, confused, but at least I seemed to be welcome here.

"What are your names?" I asked.

But they had already run off, laughing and talking loudly. The large boy ran timidly behind them. I heard a sound of something moving, and I turned. I saw they had opened one of the planes on the left wall.

"How did—" I started.

The plane slammed back into place so loudly that I flinched, bringing my hands toward my ears. It wasn't that loud, only startling, but it was loud enough to echo around the whole cavern. I could hear now that the ceiling was about three times my height, lower than I expected.

I heard a laugh in the voice of the girl who had spoken. I turned back to her. She had a big face, I thought. A big mouth, maybe. Straightish hair, and long. Yellow, maybe? Or maybe it was only because it reflected the light back well.

I don't know if it was her voice or her face, but something immediately gave me the impression that she liked to break things and set fires.

The girl laughed. "Oh, yeah, we're fine. Aika, right?"

"Yep," a second girl said. She was a little smaller and wore bright pink clothing. "What's your name again?"

"Luchia," the first girl said, "and we're going to be best friends."

What was it in her voice that made me flinch back?

"What an idiot," Luchia whispered to Aika. "Can't even look in the right direction."

They were already on the opposite side of the room, one of them moving in a strange, patterned step-jump that I thought was recklessly brave unless they knew this space very well. I heard them move around a large, rectangular object in the very center of the room. I knew I would not be able to catch up to see how they opened the plane.

I looked back at the front of the room. The man was still there. I made my way toward him.

"Kid," the man said, "you'll want to get settled in your room. You'll want to claim a bed before the other boys decide which one is yours."

I did not understand what the man had said. "Your name is Pelus, right?"

"Yes," the man said.

I smiled to make my voice lighter and friendlier. "I'm Kimi," I said. "Nice to meet you."

"Don't waste your time greeting me," Pelus said. "I'm just a guard."

I hesitated, thrown off by his grumbled voice. "I think there's been a mistake, Pelus. I'm honored that you've given me a place to rest, and your Light is very beautiful, but I'm going to be missed back home if I don't return. And it seems like you aren't very happy about me being here, so I can leave, and I won't come back. I'll tell everyone else that you don't want to be disturbed."

"They think you will come back with an army of shadows to destroy our Light," Pelus said flatly.

I blinked. "Huh? No. We won't hurt your Light. I was only curious. But it's too bright for me."

"You have no idea, kid."

Pelus's voice surprised me again.

"Listen, kid," Pelus said. "You're not going out there again, and you've got to get used to it fast. This is your home now for the next year."

"A year?" I blurted.

"One year," Pelus repeated. "It will take that long for you to learn, if you can."

I flinched. "I'll learn whatever I have to. But after a year, can I leave then?"

"You can dream of it, kid."

"But can I leave then?" I asked.

"See what happens. Might want to claim a bed right now."

I did not understand what he meant. I looked at the planes, but they were all closed right now, and I suspected Pelus would not be willing to teach me how they opened.

I heard Pelus mumble something.

I paced the room a little more, trying to get my eyes used to the light. If I squinted I could see enough to see the large object in the center of the room.

How long would I just be pacing this room? Should I ask Pelus how the planes opened?

The door behind Pelus opened, and several people came in. Six, I think, if I counted the footsteps right.

"Pelus," a familiar voice said. He was the same person who'd pulled me out of my hideaway. "Get the kids out of their rooms for the evening meal."

Pelus wordlessly went to the plane where the boys had gone in, and he knocked. "Evening meal!" he barked. The plane opened as he lumbered to the plane the girls had gone through, but it opened before he finished crossing the room.

I could catch glimpses of some of the new people. They were all adults. One was very large, but that was all I could tell of him. One woman had long hair.

One of them came up to me.

"Hey kid," the man said, "you look like you're feeling lost."

I looked at him. He was an ugly man, I thought, with stringy brown hair, a bulging forehead, and haggard gray eyes that were barely opaque. There was something friendly in his voice, though, and in his face, and it made my mind forget what it had thought before of him.

"Yeah, I guess I am," I said. I motioned. "There's so much...light." I laughed self-consciously. "For lack of a better word. So much light and so much sound."

"It must be strange to you," the man said. "You grew up out there without the Light, didn't you?"

"Yeah, I did," I said.

"Maybe it's a lucky thing," the man said. "Light is different when you don't need it the way we do."

"Maybe," I said. "I mean, I know darkness is bad."

"It doesn't have to be," the man said. "I think you said that the darkness makes you feel safe. The Light sustains us and makes us safe too, but it shouldn't be invading into your shadows."

I looked up at him.

He smiled. He had a broad, friendly smile, and it carried a warmth into his voice. "My name is Burgiss. What's yours?"

Burgiss. What an ugly name.

"Kimi," I said.

"Kimi," he said. "Well, Kimi, your first lesson is this. When someone talks to you, always make eye contact. Look them in the face. Otherwise, they will think you aren't listening."

"Oh," I said. "We usually turn our ears to people when they talk. I guess because they can't see if we're looking at them."

"That makes sense to me," Burgiss said, "but while you're here, you have to learn how to live like the people of the Light. And I know it's not easy, but it will help you manage here in the long run."

"I know," I said. "Pelus says I have a year to learn."

Burgiss was quiet for a beat. "Yes," he said flatly. "You have a year. But," he added, warmth returning to his voice, "first you need to settle in. You've had a long day. And we don't start lessons until tomorrow."

I puzzled. "Are you my teacher?"

"I'm happy to teach you if you wish," Burgiss said. "That's what we're doing this afternoon, matching teachers to students."

"Burgiss," Pelus urged, "if you keep talking, neither you nor the kid will eat."

"Oh!" Burgiss laughed. "Sorry, Kimi. Let's join the others."

I followed Burgiss, staring in confusion. Everyone was by the big object in the center of the room, sitting on chairs.

"Are you as stupid as you look?" a voice said. "Sit in that chair."

I assumed the smaller objects were chairs. I maneuvered around it.

"Don't be harsh, Dorin," Burgiss criticized next to me.

"If he can't even figure out what a chair is," the voice said, "he's not going to make it here."

"We have chairs," I said. "But we usually sit on mats when we eat."

"We sit in chairs here," Dorin said.

So, obligingly, I sat in the chair. I didn't dare move, though. I didn't want to do something else wrong already.

A voice spoke, the voice of the man who had pulled me out of my hiding place. I saw that while most of us were by the table, he stood away from it.

"All of you are here because you were selected for our retraining program," the man said, "and all of you know what you did to earn it."

"Yeah, and it was fun," one of the boys said.

The man cleared his throat loudly.

"Do not interrupt," Dorin said.

"If you make use of your time here," the man said, "you will come out of this experience as people you will be proud to be. You will walk in the good graces of the Light."

I heard Burgiss shift next to me.

"The adults who sit with you will be your teachers," the man said. "Make good use of the rest of this day to speak with them. Choose your mentor wisely, and they will help you to become the person you are capable of being.

"I will leave you to speak, and I will see you again in a year's time."

He stepped away, and chatter began. I flinched. The voices were not loud on their own, but cumulatively, they were. It wasn't loud enough to hurt exactly, although it was close to hurting. Still, it was like having bright light shining straight into your eyes, except it was sound projected straight into my ears. The high ceiling and distant walls reflected the sounds back. My surroundings sounded distorted, much smaller than they actually were, and much larger. I covered my ears, and the room started to sound the right size.

"You'll need your hands for eating," Burgiss told me.

I pulled my hands away.

Burgiss passed something to me. "Take something from the basket and pass it along."

The basket felt strange to me, light and heavily textured. I could see an opening and reached in. My hand found something and pulled it out, placing it on my plate. I held the basket to my other side, and someone took it.

Next was a bowl. I found the spoon, pouring whatever was in it onto my plate. There was one other bowl.

"You can eat now," Burgiss whispered to me.

I reached for something on my plate. My fingers met the sauce from the second bowl first, but eventually they found something solid. I took a bite.

I heard snickering.

"I'm sorry," Burgiss said. "I forgot you didn't know. There's cutlery next to you for eating."

I stared blankly, trying to look beside me. There was more sound than I was used to now, and I was having trouble hearing vibrations amid the chatter.

Burgiss picked something up from beside the plate, pressing one object into one of my hands and another object into the other of my hands.

"Now copy me," Burgiss said.

I saw him moving, and I heard something scrape, but the motions were so small I did not understand.

"Oh good Light!" someone said. "What an idiot!"

"I'll show you tomorrow," Burgiss said.

I felt ashamed. What had I done to already have disappointed Burgiss?

Still, I was hungry, so I ate piece by piece, dipping into the strange sauce and trying to ignore the laughter. The food tasted strange. It wasn't bad—or, more, it was too unfamiliar for me to decide it was bad—but it was strange.

"I think we've all figured out who we're mentoring," Dorin said.

"I think so too," another voice said.

"Then let's let the kids settle in and get some sleep," Pelus said. "Start lessons in the morning."

"We can do that," another voice agreed.

In the time it took me to stand up, the other kids had run off, and I heard the doors close.

"Don't we have to clean up?" I asked.

"No," Burgiss said. "Not this time."

"At least he's polite," someone mumbled.

"Oh come on!" I heard the larger boy whining near one of the planes. "Let me in!"

"What's the password?" a muffled voice said.

"I don't know!" the larger boy said.

"Let him in," Pelus said.

"Oh, they're still here," the muffled voice said. The plane opened, and the larger boy went in.

"That's where I'm supposed to sleep," I said, "right?"

"Yes," Burgiss said.

I was tired, I realized.

"How do I get in?" I asked.

"You don't know how to use a door?" Burgiss asked.

"What's a door?" I asked.

"This is a door," Burgiss said. "You see this knob? You hold it like this. Now twist it."

I did.

"Push it while you have it turned," Burgiss said.

I did, and I stared in amazement as the door opened.

"Do all doors work that way?" I asked.

"Yes," Burgiss said.

The door closed.

"Including the door out?" I asked.

"Well, not that one," Burgiss said. "We keep that one locked. There's a mechanism in the knob so it won't turn."

I felt my face fall.

"The first day is hard," Burgiss said sympathetically. "You share that with everyone here. No one wants to be here."

"Then why are we here?" I asked.

"Because," Burgiss explained, "this is where we bring youths who don't understand how to live here. Usually, they get themselves into trouble by committing a crime, but we also bring outsiders here, the rare times they come here."

"But I don't want to stay," I said. "I promised I'd go right back. I can tell them not to go here, and then we'll leave you alone."

Burgiss was quiet a moment. "They want to teach you how to live here because they know this place is strange to you."

"But I don't have to know," I said. "I don't plan to stay."

"Still," Burgiss said, a little too flatly, "give it the best chance that you can."

I grabbed the knob, turning and pushing. It didn't move. I pushed harder. It moved an inch and swung back shut.

"Let him in," Burgiss said.

The door swung open so quickly I almost fell. The boy behind it looked back at me with a mean smile.

"If they give you any more trouble," Burgiss told me, "tell me in the morning. If it gets too bad, there will be someone out here during the night just in case. You can come out to talk to them."

"Alright," I said.

I went in, and the boy closed the door quickly.

# 2

It was not as bright in here, but it was still bright. At least I did not have to squint. I could see that there were two bunk beds, the top and bottom connected by a ladder. I knew some families back home that used similar bunk beds, but that wasn't the norm. They looked less friendly than my usual sleeping mat, and I wasn't sure if it was only because they were unfamiliar. The boy with a large build was on the top of the one in the back, crunched as much as possible. The other two boys were still down here.

"You didn't pick your bed yet," the tousle-haired boy said. "You should have picked one. Marvus has already picked his bed."

I glanced at the heavy-set boy, presumably Marvus.

"So," the first boy said, "pick yours."

I could hear the insincerity in his voice. Still, I glanced at the beds.

"They took the—" Marvus started.

"Shut up!" the boy snapped.

I heard a place on the floor where the sound softened. When I felt with my foot I touched cloth. I lay down on that.

The three boys stared at me, dumbfounded.

"No, stupid!" the smaller boy said. "You have to pick a bed! Not the rug!"

"Well, which beds did you pick?" I asked. "I don't care."

"We're not going to tell you until you pick."

I rolled my eyes and pointed to the one below Marvus.

"No," the first boy said. "That's my bed."

I pointed to the top bunk of the set nearer the door.

"No," the second boy said. "That's mine."

I shrugged and started to climb into the remaining bed.

The first boy pulled me away gruffly. "No, that's my bed!"

The second boy laughed.

"You can't have two beds," I said.

"Pick a bed," the first boy said.

"Then I'll pick the floor," I said.

The boy pushed me onto the bunk under Marvus's.

I leapt up immediately. The bed was hard.

The two boys laughed.

I pulled the blankets aside. There were three lumpy bags underneath.

"What are you doing stealing our stuff?" the first boy asked, yanking his bag away. "You just got here and you're already stealing?"

"Yeah, are you a kleptomaniac?" the second boy asked, grabbing another bag.

I pulled out the third bag gingerly. It was deceptively light. I looked up at Marvus.

"Hey, Marvus, look," the tousle-haired boy said.

I held it up. "I'm guessing that's yours."

Marvus nodded, reaching for it. As he picked it up, though, he gasped. He looked, and he looked at the small boy. "Hey! That's mine!"

The small boy laughed in a way that made my blood boil.

Marvus climbed down, running to him.

"Marvus," the tousle-haired boy purred, "you know why you got here. Do you want to get into trouble again for the same thing on day one?"

Marvus stopped. "Can I have my stuff back, Jaim?"

"You can have it in the morning," the small boy, presumably Jaim, said.

Marvus hesitated. "Then-then I'm not giving you your stuff back."

"Okay by me," Jaim said.

Marvus seemed frozen.

There are not many things that tick me off. Life's too short to get angry too often. But this was my breaking point.

"Hey," I said. "Give the man his stuff back."

"What's it to you, outsider?" Jaim sneered.

I reached for it. Jaim pulled it away. The tousle-haired boy grabbed me and shoved me hard. I hit the ground. It didn't hurt yet, not much anyway, but I knew it would the next day.

"Leave him alone," Marvus protested feebly, stepping between me and the boys.

I stood up.

"What's here that you want anyway?" Jaim asked.

"My clothes," Marvus said, "and something my sister made for me. She calls it a medallion, but it's not really—it's-it's just tinfoil."

"Oh, living Light," the tousle-haired boy said.

"Fine," Jaim said. "Give me my stuff and I'll give you yours. None of those clothes will fit me anyway."

Marvus handed the bag back. For a moment, I didn't think Jaim would hand Marvus back his bag, but then he did.

Marvus looked in his bag. "Where is it?"

"Where's what?" Jaim asked.

"Where's my medallion?" Marvus asked.

"Give it back to him," I said.

"I don't have it," Jaim said, hands spread.

"But—" Marvus said.

"You can look for it in the morning," the tousle-haired boy said.

Marvus was still a moment. Then, silently, he went back to the bed, climbing up the ladder. I heard the ladder creak dangerously under his feet, and the bed groaned as he climbed on. He searched through his bag three more times.

"Well?" the tousle-haired boy said. "We're supposed to go to bed, outsider."

How strange, I thought, that everyone slept at the same time. Were we supposed to do that? It sure seemed that way.

I didn't want to give him any sense of superiority. But what was I going to do? I went to my bed, but I waited until they climbed into their beds before climbing into mine.

"You really showed him, Braghin," Jaim said.

The tousle-haired boy laughed in response.

Well, at least I knew everyone's name now. I doubted I'd remember by morning.

Eventually, the light faded a little, but not enough. There was a red tinge to the room, and I didn't like it. I had that same sense as in my hiding place that the light was invading in. I closed my eyes but could still see the red through my eyelids.

The bed was strange. It was softish but lumpy, sagging in weird places. I missed the mossy mats I used to sleep on. The ground might have been hard, but those mats softened the ground just enough. There wasn't much sound, and I couldn't reach to tap a sound. Sometimes someone shifted, but the beds stifled the sound. I found myself nostalgic for the sound-echoes of my home, for the shapes I knew. I missed this bulge where the cave wall started to turn to ceiling, just low enough that a person could bump their head if they stood too fast. How much it had annoyed me before. I missed being able to hear where my relatives slept. And then there was the scent. It smelled like strangers.

I heard a whimper, and at first I thought it was from me. But when I heard a second, I could feel that my throat was still. I realized it came from above me.

I'd never misplaced a sound like that before.

I didn't fall asleep for a long time, and I never stayed asleep. I covered my eyes with a blanket, but it didn't fully block the light. And the bed felt too strange to my body. But I did slowly begin to drift in and out of consciousness as my mind tried to sleep.

I heard creaks from the ladder. I started to wake, then fell back into a haze.

"Hey," I heard.

I didn't respond.

"Psst, hey!" I heard again from above. "I'm sorry. I don't know your name. Uh, can you open your eyes?"

I opened my eyes, dreading. Marvus was beside me.

"Can we switch beds?"

I blinked.

"Listen, I'm sorry," Marvus said. "I didn't want the top bunk. I'm scared it's going to break. I was just scared of them."

I blinked. "Why are you scared?"

Marvus looked embarrassed. "Um, I mean—"

"You look pretty strong," I said.

Marvus seemed to shrink into himself. "I mean, I am. People usually think I'm fat, but I'm not. But that's why I'm in trouble. That's why I'm here." He swallowed. "I'm not a bad kid. Not really. I just did something stupid, and I forgot my strength."

I considered. Marvus seemed okay. He seemed more scared than mean. "Um, yeah, sure."

"Thanks," Marvus said.

I rolled out of bed, and he climbed in. Only then did I think maybe I'd made a stupid mistake. And suddenly my gut told me I had. I looked back at him.

"What's your name, again?" Marvus asked.

"Kimi," I said.

"I'm Marvus," Marvus said.

"Yeah," I said.

"And, uh, sorry they played that prank on you. I didn't know."

"Yeah," I said, "you didn't seem to."

He smiled shyly, pulling the blankets over himself.

I didn't hear anything from the other two boys, so I quietly climbed the ladder. The ladder made almost no sound under my feet.

I still hesitated before climbing into the top bunk. It was strange being so high up, and that part made me nervous. But aside from the warmth of the bed, nothing seemed out of place. I soon fell into a doze.

—

The next morning, I ached all over, and I still felt tired. My bruises had slowly felt a little worse through the night. I could not tell how long I'd been asleep, if I'd been asleep. But now the light seemed to be brighter and bluer, and sleep was impossible.

I heard my ladder creak and jumped. I relaxed when I saw it was just Marvus.

"It's time to get up," Marvus whispered. "If we get dressed quickly we can be in the main room before they get up."

I hadn't thought before, but I only had the clothes I was wearing. My parents were appalled by the scent of my clothes after the end of a day. If this was all I had for a year, it would be too appalling even for me.

Marvus had climbed down, though, and was getting dressed. Braghin and Jaim were still blinking. Marvus was pulling his pants on as fast as he could.

I didn't have to wait really, but I already had a soft spot for Marvus. So, I waited until he was ready to bolt out the door. I followed.

"Hey!" Braghin protested. "Close the door behind you, you animals!"

I looked back in surprise. Someone was pushing the door closed.

"I thought they closed themselves," I said.

Marvus looked at me in surprise. "No, they don't."

We waited.

"What do we do now?" I asked.

"I don't know," Marvus said.

We stood awkwardly for a while before Marvus went to the table. I joined.

"You can help with breakfast if you are awake," someone grunted.

I looked up. I recognized his voice. He was one of the adults from yesterday.

"Yes, but how?" Marvus said.

"Don't be lazy," the man said.

Marvus flinched. "Y-yes sir, but...I don't know how..."

"Where do we go?" I asked.

"Stop asking questions and go help."

Marvus and I looked at each other.

The adult sighed sharply, and I heard a scratching sound. I thought I saw his hand move.

"I'm recording this," the man said. "You're already starting in a bad place, boys. You are starting as troublemakers."

"We just don't know where to go is all," I said.

"Kimi—" Marvus started nervously.

"Don't talk back!" the man scolded, scratching.

"I wasn't talking back!" I spluttered. "We just didn't know—"

"Kimi," Marvus said urgently. "It's okay."

"No, it's not!" I protested.

"Kimi," Marvus said, "we'll get into more trouble if we argue."

"Huh?" I asked. "But we're already in trouble."

"But—"

I heard one of the doors creak and turned. Someone was carrying something.

"Help him," the man said.

Marvus all but scampered over. I tapped to hear where the table was. I heard more scratching from the man as I found my way around.

"Thank you, Marvus," the person carrying things said.

I recognized the person's voice as Burgiss's and felt embarrassed. I made my way around the table, catching my toe briefly on the leg of one of the chairs. By the time I was around, Burgiss and Marvus had reached the table and were putting the items down.

"Good morning, Kimi," Burgiss said.

"Hi, Burgiss," I greeted.

"You picked your worst student yet, Burgiss," the man said. "He's lazy as well as stupid."

"I'm not," I protested.

Burgiss brought a hand to my shoulder. "Ossik, they haven't been assigned chores yet. He isn't supposed to be awake yet."

"If he's up, he should be helping you," Ossik said. "You know the rules as well as anyone."

"He doesn't yet," Burgiss said.

"I wanted to help," I said. "I just didn't know where I was supposed to go."

Burgiss's hand moved from my shoulder. "That door there."

I blinked.

Ossik laughed. "Oh living Light."

"Do you see my hand?" Burgiss asked.

"Um..." I said.

"You can't see," Burgiss realized.

"I can," I said. "I mean, I can see your face right now. Most of it."

"Most of it?" Burgiss repeated. "Okay, I'm moving my hand. Don't move your head. Tell me when you can see it."

Time passed silently. I saw blurs, but I knew that wasn't what Burgiss meant. I waited until the blur materialized into a hand as it passed Burgiss's left cheekbone.

"I see it," I said.

Burgiss dropped his hand.

"How did you find your way here?"

"I listened," I said.

"No wonder you had so much trouble last night," Burgiss said.

"You pick your students well, Burgiss," Ossik said. "This one can't even see the Light!"

"That means nothing," Burgiss said.

"You know you're doomed, boy," Ossik said. "Burgiss has a sixth sense for—"

"Burgiss," Pelus's voice came, "they're asking for you."

Burgiss sighed in exasperation. "Fine. Kimi, don't let him push you around."

I heard his footsteps leave, and I heard the door to the boys' bedroom open.

"Might as well take your seats, boys," Pelus grunted to us.

Marvus and I quickly found our seats.

Burgiss came out with more items, which he placed on the table. I heard someone else come in. Two people, I realized, when I heard the asynchrony of their steps. One had a heavier, slower step. The other had a faster, lighter one.

One person hammered at the boys' room. "Boys, get up!" I recognized Dorin's voice.

"Girls, get up!" a woman's voice barked. Her voice made me jump.

I heard people moving slowly, slumping to the table. Bowls were passed around, and this time, Burgiss helped me to take things from the bowls. People ate silently. Because they were tired, I thought.

"Kimi," Burgiss said, "can you see enough to find the cutlery?"

"Yeah," I said, tilting my head. It was small, but eventually I saw them enough to grab them.

"Can you tell that they are different?" Burgiss asked.

"Yes," I said. "I've used spoons back home. I've used knives, but usually that's for preparing food, not for eating it. And I don't know what this thing with three points is."

"That's a fork," Burgiss said. "You hold it like this."

He positioned the fork into my hand, and then he positioned the knife.

"So you use the fork like another hand," Burgiss said. "Or like a spear. You're using it to pick up food. The knife you use to cut food into a size that fits into your mouth. Does that make sense?"

"Yeah, that makes sense," I replied.

I tried to copy the directions Burgiss had given me. Moving the fork felt strange though.

"It's like an extension of your finger," Burgiss said.

It took me three tries to stab something on my plate. I then started cutting at it. Someone laughed.

"You cut it like you're butchering it!" a woman's voice said.

"They're both extensions of your fingers, Kimi," Burgiss said.

He repositioned the knife in my hand.

"Try that way," Burgiss said. "Think of it like it's a way of elongating your finger."

I tried. It was such an awkward way to hold something. It took me several tries to cut something. But finally, I figured it out, and I brought whatever I had cut to my mouth. The bland flavor and leathery texture was hardly a reward.

Still, I was hungry, and I was supposed to learn, so I kept eating. Little by little, I started to grasp the skill. But a few bites later, everyone else had finished eating, and they started to chatter. The sound started to hurt, and I felt myself shrinking back.

"Can you be quiet while he finishes eating?" Burgiss asked.

If anything, they were louder.

"Quiet down," Pelus said firmly.

The chatter died down enough that I could resume eating. Even I noticed how painfully long it took for me to finish.

"You may now go with your mentors," Dorin said, "and your mentors will decide your lessons. You will be given your chore schedules, and you will be expected to follow them."

"What is a chorskejul?" I asked.

I heard snickering.

"Chore ske-joo-wull," Dorin sounded out. "You will be given the schedule to read."

I frowned. I didn't know what that meant, but I was not sure I wanted to ask.

"I'll explain it to you in a moment, Kimi," Burgiss said.

"Go start your lessons," Dorin said. "Braghin, follow me."

"Kimi," Burgiss said, his voice low, "we're going to go to a side room so you have some quiet."

I followed him to the door before the boys' bedroom. When the door closed, the silence was welcome. I tapped my foot, listening, but there was nothing of interest here: a few crates, one bed, and little else.

Burgiss sank down onto the ground, and I sat next to him. My arm hurt when I touched the floor, so I brought it up a moment before easing myself down.

"Are you alright?" Burgiss asked.

"Yeah," I said.

"Did they hurt you?"

"Not much," I said.

"Then they did," Burgiss said. "Who was it?"

"Braghin and Jaim," I said.

"But not Marvus," Burgiss said. "I'm not surprised. Marvus shouldn't be in this program either. Neither of you should."

"Why is Marvus here?" I asked.

"That's for him to tell you," Burgiss said. He sighed. "I'll talk to Dorin and Ossik. Maybe we can move your sleeping quarters in here. You and Marvus if possible."

"That would be good," I said.

"I can't promise you anything," Burgiss said, "but I'll try."

"Thanks," I said.

"Kimi," Burgiss said, "for future, do not ask the others questions. They will not understand, and they will only mock you. Ask them to me."

"I understand," I said.

Burgiss was quiet.

"What is my first lesson?"

Burgiss smiled wryly. "That is a good question. Usually, it's very clear what a student has to learn here. You probably already know what your—"

The door opened, and I jumped.

"Pelus, Marvus, come in," Burgiss said.

"You don't have the authority to keep us out," Pelus grunted, closing the door.

Burgiss chuckled. "No."

"So, you might want a grunt or two to keep the others out," Pelus said. "Unless you want to try teaching in the broom closet."

"Thank you, Pelus," Burgiss said.

Pelus and Marvus sat down near the door.

"You chose Marvus," Burgiss said.

"He's too quiet," Pelus said. "They'll devour him."

"I didn't know you had a soft spot for the shy ones," Burgiss said.

"That's because last time the guardian of lost causes found the shy kid first," Pelus said pointedly.

Burgiss laughed.

I was confused. "Guardian of lost causes?"

"He's making fun of me," Burgiss said.

"Do they think I'm a lost cause?" I asked.

"You're starting very far behind," Burgiss said, "but you learn fast. You already know how to use a fork even though you've never seen one before."

"I promised before that I would learn everything I had to by the end of the year," I said.

"That's not what makes you a lost cause," Pelus said. "It's convincing them that you learned."

Burgiss looked sober. "That will be the hard part. But Kimi, you will do it, and you will do it by mastering our way of life so well that they have to argue. Are you prepared for that?"

The idea should have daunted me. Burgiss's tone of voice should have made me think. But I did not think twice.

"Yeah," I said firmly.

# 3

"First," Burgiss said, "let me give you your schedule. I know it will be pointless. I don't know if you can see it well enough to read it."

I heard Pelus murmuring to Marvus behind me. He was saying something similar.

Burgiss handed me something flat. It had ink marks on it in different shapes, but the shapes were blurry. I pulled it closer to my eye. When it was an inch from my eye I could start to make out the shapes.

Burgiss caught my hand and pulled it back.

"If you can't see it," Burgiss said, "it's not your fault, and I will argue for you until I have no breath."

"He is not exaggerating, boy," Pelus said. "Your mentor is as tenacious as titanium."

"And Marvus," Burgiss said, "you are in good hands. Pelus has a temper as smooth as glass."

"But not so brittle," Pelus said.

"No," Burgiss said. "Your mentor's also better at metaphors."

Marvus laughed weakly.

"Kimi," Burgiss said, "since you cannot see the schedule, I can explain it to you. There's six of you, so every six days, you trade off. Today you weren't assigned any meals, but tomorrow you are assigned to help make lunch. Two days after, you are assigned to help make dinner. And then two days after, breakfast. I can remind you when it is your turn, and we'll be working together."

"That makes sense," I said.

"Every other day," Burgiss said, "you will set the table and clean, so we will do that during lunch today. Two days from today, we'll do the same for dinner."

"Okay," I said.

"I know what happened is not your fault," Pelus was saying behind me. "Most of us know. But you are bigger than most people, and at your age it is hard to know your own strength. I was put through this retraining program for almost the same reason."

"You were retrained?" I asked.

"Kimi—" Burgiss started.

"We all were," Pelus said. "That's how they pick the mentors. They pick from the people who successfully completed the retraining program."

I turned to Burgiss. "You did this program?"

"Yes," Burgiss replied.

"Why?" I asked.

"It's complicated," Burgiss said. "I can tell you when you have a better grasp of your own studies. This is not skewed in your favor, Kimi. Most people here need to learn one or two skills, five at most, and then maybe a bit of math or science or a career skill. You have to learn everything, but you especially need to learn how to understand the Light."

"We'll try not to distract you," Pelus said.

"It might help him to have a peer who isn't his enemy," Burgiss said.

"Are you going to put my student through what you went through?" Pelus asked.

Burgiss flinched. "That's harsh, Pelus."

"It is what you are suggesting," Pelus said.

"It's not what I meant," Burgiss said. "But...I see your point."

"What?" I asked.

"It—don't worry about it," Burgiss said. "It was a bad idea. Let's start with what is the Light. Or...no, that won't make sense yet."

"He's smart enough, Burgiss," Pelus said. "Tell him."

"Let's start with our society's structure," Burgiss said. "You already saw...what did you see when you first arrived?"

"I don't know," I admitted. "I saw three people on a platform and a bunch of people watching them, and there was a kid kneeling."

"It was a ceremony," Burgiss said. "The three people you saw are our council. They are in charge of our home. They lead ceremonies, enact laws, and make sure everything in the background works so that life can go on. Everything in the background is mostly the Light."

"And what is the Light?" I asked.

"The Light is everything to us," Burgiss said. "It's a structure woven into every part of our home. Every place you are able to see is penetrated by the Light. Obviously, we depend on our eyesight, so we need the Light to see. But the Light also allows our plants to grow so that we can eat, and it provides warmth where we grow warm-weather plants. And perhaps most importantly, it creates environments that allow us to purify our water and breakdown waste products. It gives us stability." He paused. "I'm curious, actually. How do you live without the Light? I know you can't see."

"No, we listen," I said. "You can hear, right? You hear what I'm saying."

"I hear you, yes," Burgiss said. "But how does that let you, for example, walk across a room without hurting yourself?"

"Oh, I listen for the echoes," I said. "So, let's say I don't know where Pelus is. So, I'll do this." I clapped twice, loudly. "So, you can hear it, right? The sound goes soft when it hits you or Pelus because you're soft. But you can hear the echo off the walls and the floor and the crates. It's a little softer off the crates, but the echo is strong when it hits stone or water. Or, better, if I tap the floor—" I slapped the floor twice with my palm. "—then I hear the vibration down the floor a little too. Or more, you can feel it in your feet if you pay attention."

"That's why you're barefoot," Burgiss said.

"What?" I asked.

"You aren't wearing shoes," Burgiss said.

"What are shoes?" I asked.

"You put them on your feet," Burgiss said.

"He'll need to get used to wearing them," Pelus said.

"We can wait until he knows his surroundings," Burgiss said. "It sounds like that's how you know where you are."

"Yeah, it is," I said.

"So, let's wait on that," Burgiss said. "We have a year. Let's get everything else out of the way first.

"Kimi, you also need to know that the Light...because we are so dependent on the Light, we are fearful of darkness. Without the Light, our crops cannot grow, our water will be unclean, and we will be sightless. We would be lost. So when you said that not all darkness is bad, I understand what you were saying, but that touched on our worst fears."

"I wasn't going to hurt your Light," I said. "I was only curious about it."

"I know you weren't," Burgiss said gently. "No one thinks you were going to harm us. The Light must be nearly as scary to you as the dark is to us."

"Not really," I said. "But noise is. I can't hear where I am in the big room."

"I can see that," Burgiss said. "But for future, for now, don't talk about the dark. Don't mention the dark, especially in a positive way."

"I won't," I said. "I'll try not to. But is there a place I can get away from the light at all? I think it's giving me a headache."

"There isn't," Burgiss said sympathetically. "Even when we sleep, the Light does not dim fully."

"Yeah, I saw that," I said.

"Be patient with yourself," Burgiss said. "You know the most important things now, and if you keep them in the back of your mind, you'll learn everything else."

I was not certain I believed him.

"Who was the kid who was kneeling?" I asked.

"That...that can wait for another day. It's complicated."

I heard Pelus grunt.

"By the way," Burgiss said, "are these your only set of clothes?"

"Yes," I said.

"I'll get you some more clothes tomorrow."

I can't recall that Burgiss taught me much else that day. He went over manners, mostly, and that made my head hurt more. Things like when to make eye contact, when to look away, when to shake hands, when to avoid touching, what behaviors and words were appropriate for friends and which ones suggested a romantic interest. It all blurs together now. All I remember fully was that it only made sense with enough constant light.

But after, he helped me figure out the Light people's version of chores.

"So first we need to get the plates," Burgiss said. "They're all in the kitchen."

I followed him into the door to the front right, the one before the girls' bedroom. I didn't process this room very well. It was very bright, narrow and full of metal, with strong smells and loud noises that bounced through the claustrophobic space. Something was cooking, something as strange as anything else here.

"We keep everything here," Burgiss said, pulling open a cabinet near the door. He pulled something from the side. "We'll put everything we need on this cart, and we'll bring it out."

It was arranged so neatly, with the plates and napkins on one upper shelf and the cutlery each in a different section on a lower shelf. There were more than we needed. We counted out the right amount of plates together, and the right amount of forks, spoons, knives, and napkins, and we put them all on the cart.

"Do you remember how they were set before?" Burgiss asked.

"Yeah, I remember," I said. "It's pretty much what we do back home too."

"Just make sure you fold the napkins this way," Burgiss said.

Mealtime was nothing worth mentioning, and it was the first time I got through a meal without being completely awkward. It was still too loud, and I was still too slow, but my hand was understanding how to use a fork, and I was starting to figure out how to decipher some things through the noise. It did not make the food taste any less weird.

What I didn't realize was that there were more chores after washing dishes.

"So, this small door in the back," Burgiss said, "this is where we keep the cleaning supplies."

"The one that doesn't match the rest of the doors?" I asked.

"Yes," Burgiss said.

"I was wondering why this one didn't have a door across from it," I said.

Burgiss paused, glancing at each door. "You're right. Huh. That's what's so unsettling about this room."

"You didn't notice?" I asked.

"I did," Burgiss said, "but I didn't see how...anyway, you fill this with soap and water, and you towel off the table. And after that, you can sweep the floor. And then you're finally done."

It would have been unremarkable, and over time it was. But this first time, I was surprised how much food was on the table. I wondered why they would leave it scattered in slimy landscapes rather than eat it.

Well, I thought, it was not my stomach that would be empty.

—

That night, Marvus and I both got into bed as quickly as possible to be out of the way of our two roommates.

My knee hit something that crinkled with a noise and a sensation that made the back of my neck tingle. I jumped, bopping my head on the ceiling. I groaned, rubbing at the top of my head.

"Are you okay?" Marvus asked.

"Yeah," I said.

I pulled back my blanket. There were three shiny objects there. When I first tried to pick one up, the sound of the material against my skin made me flinch back. I steeled myself and picked them up more gingerly. The objects were flimsy and felt somehow smooth and rough at the same time. They glinted bright specks of white into my eyes, like pyrite.

"What are these?" I asked.

"Let me see," Marvus said.

I handed the pieces down to him.

I heard him make a sad sound.

I looked down. He was arranging the pieces in his hand. When he finished, they seemed to form a star, with some sort of design inside.

"What happened, Marvus?" Jaim asked. "Did the weird kid do something?"

"It was you, and I know it!" Marvus yelled. "My sister made this! Why did you break it?"

"Maybe she shouldn't have made it so flimsy," Jaim said.

"She didn't make it flimsy!" Marvus protested.

"You want to fight over it?" Jaim asked.

Marvus hesitated. He whined in anger, turning over in his bed.

"Don't let that stuff poke your eye out," Jaim said.

I waited until the other two boys were in their beds before peeking down.

"Marvus?" I whispered. "I'm sorry."

Marvus didn't reply.

# 4

A few days later, the shadow-snatcher came.

Burgiss had warned me before about the shadow-snatcher, and I was ready.

"Don't be frightened," Burgiss said. "He will look scary to you, and he will speak strangely. But in his mind, he is here to help you."

"What does a shadow-snatcher do?" I asked.

"A shadow-snatcher is there to look for your shadows," Burgiss said, "and he is there to help you move on from those shadows so you can find your way toward light."

"How does he get rid of shadows?" I asked, confused.

"You tell him what your shadows are," Burgiss said.

I blinked. "Isn't a shadow just what you get if there's enough light?"

"Don't say that to him," Burgiss said quickly. "Yes, in reality, yes. Or, the way we'd say it, you get a shadow if one side of you does not have light."

"What?" I asked.

"Remember, Kimi," Burgiss said. "The Light is not just light. It's everything that is good. And shadows are the things you do wrong, or the negative thoughts in your head, the ones that you are ashamed to have even though everyone has them."

"I think I understand?" I said.

"I'm sure you do," Burgiss said. "All he wants is for you to tell him something you did wrong. He'll tell you what you have to do better, and then you are done. But Kimi, remember, you don't have to tell him anything you don't want to tell him. Others will tell you differently, but you need only tell him one thing you regret. You don't have to shatter your heart."

"Okay, yeah," I said. "I can think of something."

"It will make sense after you see it once," Burgiss said.

When the shadow-snatcher stepped through, accompanied by Dorin, I understood why Burgiss had called him "scary." Something in his walk was too smooth. His footsteps sounded too precise. I could hear his clothes rustling. He wore a white robe with long sleeves, so long they drifted to his knees. The hem nearly reached the floor. His hair was bright white.

He stepped away from Dorin so smoothly and silently that I could only think that he moved like light. Even when he opened the door to the back of the room, he moved so quietly that I almost didn't hear the door open. I did hear the nearly-silent click as it closed.

"Get in line," Dorin said. "No talking."

We were already pretty much in line.

"Try to be at the front of the line if you can," Burgiss had told me earlier. "Get it done fast. The shadow-snatcher that comes here will be briefer if you are first than if you are last."

I'd listened to his advice. I was second in line.

Aika went into the room first. The door closed.

I could hear them talking, faintly, although I could not make out the words. Or more, I willed myself not to. The man had a warm amber voice. I wanted to find that voice comforting.

The door opened, and Aika left, passing silently. No one behind me spoke. The silence unnerved me more than anything else.

I stepped in.

This room was smaller than the others, smaller than I expected, and bright. It was nearly empty except for three chairs, the middle one occupied by the shadow-snatcher. Perhaps the emptiness was what made this room feel brighter.

The shadow-snatcher did not move when I entered. He was so silent I could almost have forgotten he was there.

I did as Burgiss had told me. I sat in front of him, looking down. "Do not make eye contact with him. It is very rude to make eye-contact with a shadow-snatcher before he tells you to do so."

Up close, the man unnerved me more. He moved so slowly and deliberately, and his eyes stared so piercingly. His clothes did not have so much as a smudge. His hair was not just white: it was unnaturally white. I thought he might be wearing white paint on his face, but maybe he was only pale. A strange, toxic smell lingered around him, part chemical and part metallic.

A medallion hung from his neck, very similar to Marvus's tinfoil one except bright white and so shiny that it hurt my eyes when the barest light glinted off of it. Burgiss had let me handle a similar medallion so I would knew its shape. It was a circle with eight triangles stretching from it. Its center was open, but lines stretched inward from the center of each triangle to a smaller circle, also open in the middle.

"The shadow-snatcher wears this as part of a uniform," Burgiss had explained. "But he is not the only one. Many people have these as protection charms to ward off evil. You have to know this symbol, Kimi. Even the youngest children can draw it, and even a toddler knows what it means."

"Did your mentor explain to you why I am here?" the shadow-snatcher asked.

"Yes," I said.

"What shadow do you have right now?" the shadow-snatcher asked.

I shrugged to hide my nerves. I felt my face trying to smile.

"Do you think this is funny?" the shadow-snatcher asked.

"No," I said. "No, I think it's serious."

"Your face tells me you are lying."

"No, I smile when I'm nervous," I said. "No, the shadow

I have is I came here. I shouldn't have come here. I scared people, and that was a bad thing."

"Coming to the Light is not a shadow," the shadow-snatcher said. "The Light can help you, if you are willing."

I wasn't sure what to say.

"Tell me your shadows so I can dispel them," the shadow-snatcher said.

I tried to think. I couldn't think of anything else I regretted.

"I can't think of anything," I finally said. "I can't think of any other shadows."

"Then you are arrogant," the shadow-snatcher said.

"Huh?" I said. "No, I—"

"You come freshly to the Light from the darkness," the shadow-snatcher said, "but you say you have no shadows."

"No, it's not that I don't have any," I said quickly. "I just don't know yet. That's all."

"Look at me," the shadow-snatcher said.

I flinched. The last thing I wanted was to make eye-contact with him now. But still, I forced my neck to crane up to him. His face was a strange white blur with at least one of his eyes burning into mine. I turned slightly so that his cheekbone was in focus instead, and that took the edge from his sulfury gaze.

"Your shadow is your arrogance," the shadow-snatcher said. "You think you are above the Light. Now, I want you to say the words 'I'm sorry.'"

"Why?" I asked.

"Say them," the shadow-snatcher said.

I blinked. "I'm sorry?"

"Say them," the shadow-snatcher said, "and mean them this time."

Whatever this crazy talk was, I thought, I just had to get it over with.

"I'm sorry," I said, trying to sound like I meant it.

"Say it again," the shadow-snatcher said.

"I'm sorry," I repeated.

How many times was he going to expect me to say it? And what was I apologizing for?

"For the rest of this week," the shadow-snatcher said, "you will find opportunities to apologize so that you can work to banish this shadow. Only then will the Light find its way into your blackened heart."

"That's a bit harsh, don't you think?" I asked.

The shadow-snatcher stood so sharply that I jumped. He pointed a finger at me. "Apologize for your arrogance."

I blinked. "Um...I'm sorry. I don't know what I said that—"

"Don't explain yourself," the shadow-snatcher interrupted. "That is your arrogance, your assumption that you are right."

"I'm sorry," I said automatically.

"You may leave," the shadow-snatcher said. "And remember, apologize whenever you are asked, and whenever you can, so you can banish this deeply-rooted shadow."

"I'm sorry," I said again before standing. My feet moved faster than I expected. I slammed the door behind myself.

Marvus, who was behind me, stared.

I smiled. "Uh, your turn."

"No talking," Dorin scolded. "Go to the back of the line."

I winced. Did I have to go back a second time?

Was I supposed to say "I'm sorry" or say nothing? I opted to say nothing since Dorin was watching now.

"Bad, huh?" Aika whispered.

I glanced. "Um, yeah."

"Dorin, he's whispering to me," Aika said.

I jumped. "What—"

"Kimi, no talking," Dorin scolded.

"But—" I started.

"This is a solemn moment," Dorin interrupted. "I'll report this to your mentor."

Would the shadow-snatcher report to the mentors what he'd told me? No doubt he would.

I hated knowing what they were going to expect me to do.

"I'm sorry," I said reluctantly.

"You should be," Dorin said.

I heard Luchia giggle ahead. I felt my teeth lock together and my fists clenched.

The door opened, and the line stepped forward a space. There was something comforting about having Marvus behind me. I glanced back at Marvus to see how he was. His brow was furrowed.

"Kimi," Dorin warned.

I opened my mouth to protest. But no, I wasn't supposed to fight back. I was only supposed to apologize.

The main door opened shortly after Jaim went inside. I recognized the footstep-patterns of Ossik and Burgiss. One of the women was there too. I wasn't sure which one she was. I noticed that Burgiss kept back, away from the door but also away from everyone else, almost nearer the kitchen.

Luchia was last. When she came out, I had to admire the calm I could hear in her pace. I glimpsed her face. It was placid, her eyes cool.

The door opened again, and the shadow-snatcher stepped out.

"I have spoken with each of the students," the shadow-snatcher said. "They know what they must do to banish their shadows."

"Thank you," Dorin said. To us, he said, "you may meet with your mentors now."

"Burgiss," the shadow-snatcher said, "I have not seen you in some time."

"I see another shadow-snatcher now," Burgiss said a little too tersely.

"Have you seen one today?" the shadow-snatcher asked.

"I have," Burgiss said.

"Then next time," the shadow-snatcher said, "you should admit to the shadow of not preparing your student well."

Burgiss waited a beat. "Will you tell me what went wrong?"

"You can ask your student," the shadow-snatcher said. "If he will tell you. I am not surprised which mentor chose him."

The shadow-snatcher turned with that perfectly smooth step, all but gliding out the door that Dorin opened for him.

"I hate that man," Burgiss muttered.

I laughed.

"You could hear me from over there?" Burgiss asked.

"Yeah, I heard you," I said.

"What did you say?" Dorin asked.

"Nothing," Burgiss said.

"What did he say, boy?" Dorin asked.

"Nothing," I said.

"Then why were you laughing?" Dorin asked.

I shrugged. "Um...I'm sorry."

"Why are you apologizing?" Dorin said.

"The shadow-snatcher said to apologize," I said.

"Then you should apologize for being impudent," Dorin said.

"Was I being impudent?" I asked.

"And for questioning authority," Dorin added.

"Dorin," Burgiss eased, "I think he was only confused. Let me talk to him."

"If he's confused about the shadow-snatcher," Dorin said, "that's your fault, as the shadow-snatcher said."

"Then all the more reason for me to talk to him," Burgiss said. "Kimi, let's talk in the kitchen."

I followed him. Burgiss closed the door quietly, holding it in place a moment, before turning, his back firmly to the door. He let out an angry sigh.

"I'm sorry," I said, nervous.

"Stop apologizing," Burgiss said firmly.

I blinked, confused.

"What happened?" Burgiss said.

I hesitated. "Um...I tried saying that coming here was my shadow because I scared people."

"And that didn't work," Burgiss said. "Right?"

"Yeah," I said.

"He's not as bright as he acts," Burgiss said. "It's obvious what you were saying, but he didn't hear it. Probably because it's a kinder thing than he's thought in his life."

I blinked. "You really don't like him."

"I have some personal quarrels with him," Burgiss said.

I was afraid to ask, so I said nothing.

"So, what did you say instead?"

"I couldn't think of anything," I said. "And I tried to explain I didn't know, and he said I was arrogant and said I should apologize."

I heard Burgiss's fingers scrape against the door as they closed into a fist, then scrape again as they released. "Kimi, for future, don't tell people what the shadow-snatcher told you to do. Now they're going to take advantage of that for the next week at least, and maybe longer. I'll deflect as much of it as I can, but you're going to have to bear most of it."

"Yeah," I said, understanding.

We were quiet a moment.

"I mean," I said, "you're bearing it too. You're letting them think you trained me wrong."

"I'm not the one being retrained," Burgiss said. "I can take it. But you'll get a reputation you don't deserve."

I shrugged, not sure what else to say.

"So, I don't understand," I said. "What was so wrong about what I said?"

Burgiss looked sympathetic. "It's not something you did wrong so much as there's no way to do it right. Especially for you. You know how to live with darkness; we don't. And that makes the others distrust you more. That shadow-snatcher wanted to humiliate you. He decides for himself who carries darkness before they can explain themselves."

"He decided you carry darkness too, didn't he?" I said.

Burgiss smiled wryly. "Did I make it that obvious?"

"Yeah, you did," I said.

He laughed. "I am too stubborn for my own good. I argued with him when I was in retraining, sometimes so loudly that they heard it out here." His expression softened. "The problem is that we expect everyone to have darkness in them, but we expect it more of some people than others. And when people expect us to have darkness, whether we want to or not, we live up to those expectations." He looked me in the eye. "Which is why I expect you to do well and prove them all wrong."

"Thanks, Burgiss," I said. "So, since I couldn't think what to say this time, how should I look for shadows?"

"I wouldn't look too hard," Burgiss said. "You can always find darkness if you look hard enough, but you can obsess so much searching for shadows that you see nothing else. And sometimes, expressing some of those shadows can make them worse, not better. Better not to give them oxygen." He smiled, and I saw the mischief behind it. "Most of us keep a list of shadows in our heads. I can give you a list of mine if you want."

I startled. "Um, yeah, sure."

"I'll give it to you tomorrow," Burgiss said. "Or...wait, you can't read."

"No," I said.

"Then I'll read it to you tomorrow," Burgiss said. "And if you ever need, you can always involve me. If they ask, I'll cover for you. Just make sure it's believable. I can't pretend you gave me a black eye if it's obvious I don't have one."

"Thanks, Burgiss," I said.

"And this conversation never happened," Burgiss said.

I smiled. "Yeah, of course."

I heard the door handle turn, but it stopped mid-click. "Don't let him get you down, Kimi."

"I won't," I promise.

The door handle clicked fully, and the door creaked open.

# 5

It was not hard to keep the shadow-snatcher from getting me down. He only came once in a while. The other students, on the other hand, it was a little harder.

I remember one night that was particularly bad that week. It started that I was getting ready for bed when Jaim ran into me.

"Ouch!" Jaim said. "You hit me. Now you have to apologize."

I rolled my eyes. "I'm sorry." Anything for some quiet.

"I didn't hear you," Jaim said.

"I said it," I said.

"But I didn't hear you," Jaim said.

Braghin ran into me from behind, and I stumbled.

"Kimi, you're right in my way," he said. "Apologize."

I sighed. I was tired. It had been a really long day. It had been my first day with shoes, which had softened my footsteps, although not as much as I'd expected. My feet hurt from having to learn a new way of walking, though, and my head was hurting from trying to learn to read.

"I know it isn't fair, Kimi," Burgiss had said. "But the council told me I have to teach you this. And if it's going to be hard for you to learn, you have to learn sooner rather than later."

I already had the distinct impression that the more I learned, the more I would be expected to learn. That no matter what, I was going to fail.

Might as well avoid what small fights I could to leave myself energy for the bigger ones.

"Stop making him apologize," Marvus said.

I looked to him in surprise. He was standing firmly. But I heard the fear in the undertone of his voice.

"Did you want to fight about it, Marvus?" Braghin asked.

I heard Marvus's foot shift.

"I'm not going to fight you," Marvus said, voice shaking, "but...Kimi, you don't have to apologize for something you didn't do. It isn't fair."

I couldn't think what to say. He was right.

"He didn't apologize to you yet," Jaim said.

"Well?" Braghin asked.

Marvus was right.

"No," I said. "You ran into me. I'm not going to apologize."

Braghin came so close to me that I could smell his stale breath. "The shadow-snatcher told you to apologize."

"I don't have to apologize for things I didn't do," I replied.

Braghin stepped even closer. I resisted the urge to step back.

"Kimi—" Marvus started.

"If you aren't going to banish your shadows," Braghin said, "we'll have to beat them out for you."

I dodged his first punch. I tried to run for the door, but Jaim ran into me, throwing me off balance.

Braghin grabbed the front of my shirt, pulling me up.

"All you had to do was apologize!" Braghin said.

I blocked his punch.

"Braghin, stop!" Marvus protested.

Braghin punched me again. This time his fist met my chin.

"Um, Braghin..." Jaim started.

"What, are you scared?" Braghin asked.

"Yeah, kinda," Jaim said. "I mean, if you—if we beat him up too badly, it's going to be one of us."

"It's not going to be me," Braghin said.

"Yeah, but it could be me," Jaim said.

"We've got bum-face over there," Braghin said.

Braghin punched me again, this time in the stomach. It hurt. I felt nauseous.

And then Braghin suddenly came away from me, and I fell to the floor again. He yelped, landing so heavily against his bed that I heard the bed creak.

I sat up. Marvus was standing near me. Jaim was open-mouthed. The bed was creaking as Braghin sat up.

"You're not supposed to punch people!" Braghin spluttered.

"I couldn't take it anymore," Marvus said.

"That's what got you here!" Jaim said.

"That's not what got me here," Marvus said. "That's why I threw him on a bed."

"I'm going to tell them you threw me," Braghin said.

His feet hit the floor.

"If you do that—" Marvus said. Braghin stopped. "If you do that I will tell them how badly you were beating up Kimi."

I heard how much Marvus's voice trembled. I think he was more scared than I was.

Braghin stepped.

"Braghin," Jaim stammered, "let's—let's not."

"Are you scared?" Braghin asked again.

"Yeah, I kinda am," Jaim said. "Not of him, but...let's—we can leave it for tonight."

"Fine," Braghin said.

I heard them moving away, and then Marvus's heavy steps came to me. He reached down and pulled me to my feet.

"Are you alright?" he asked.

"Yeah, I'm alright," I said. "Thanks."

"I couldn't stand it any longer," Marvus said.

I gave him what I hoped was a grateful smile.

—

The next morning, I could feel the soreness in my jaw, my arm, and especially my stomach. I suppressed a groan as I got up. Still, as was my habit now, I got ready swiftly and got out the door before the others woke up. Marvus was only a couple of footsteps behind me.

Dorin was the first mentor to arrive.

"Did Marvus punch you?" Dorin asked.

I blinked. "What? No."

"How did you get that bruise on your face?" he asked.

I could feel it throbbing on my chin.

But, I thought, I couldn't tell him. He wouldn't believe me. He'd say it was Marvus.

And if he did? Then Marvus's bargain last night would be in vain. It would only work again if we didn't tattle on them this time.

"I, uh, I stumbled," I said. "First day with shoes."

Dorin grunted.

"I'm sorry," I said.

Dorin made a sound of puzzlement. "I don't think you are understanding what the shadow-snatcher told you."

I heard the bedroom door open, and I heard Braghin's reluctant footsteps. It was his turn to set the table.

Pelus was the next person to say something.

"What happened to your face?" Pelus asked.

"I tripped on something," I lied, my voice carrying the lie more easily this time. "New shoes."

"Hmm," he replied.

Burgiss was the last to arrive. We were already seated when he came in.

"You're late," Pelus said.

"Yeah, I know," Burgiss said.

I blinked. He sounded grouchy.

"What kept you?" Pelus asked.

"Nothing," Burgiss said. "Don't worry about it."

He sat next to me.

"Are you okay?" I asked.

"Yeah, I'm fine," Burgiss said, his voice more friendly now.

The bruised side of my face was turned away from him. That was a good thing, I thought. I could wait as long as possible before he noticed if he was already upset about something.

For once, it was silent as we ate, so silent that I could hear every click of every fork on every plate, and I heard the myriad clinking echoes around the room like water drops in a cavern. The sound was almost comforting. Almost like home.

I'd managed not to be homesick for a long time. The thought suddenly made it worse, and the pain in my stomach had already made it hard to eat. Especially this strange, foreign food that I still could not name.

I put down my knife and fork.

"Are you okay?" Burgiss asked.

"Yeah," I lied.

"What happened?" Burgiss asked sharply.

I blinked.

"I can see the bruise on your face," Burgiss said. "What happened?"

"Nothing," I said. "I just tripped on something. My chin hit the bedpost."

"Who punched you?" Burgiss demanded.

I hesitated. "N-no one did."

"Burgiss," Pelus said, "it can wait."

"But—" Burgiss started.

"You can talk to him later," Pelus said.

Burgiss said nothing. Eventually, I heard the clicking of his fork against his plate. It sounded too heavy, and I heard the tines scrape the ceramic. If I looked his way, I saw that he was hunched.

I tried to eat. I managed some nibbles.

As soon as the meal was over, and as soon as Ossik and Jaim began cleaning up, Burgiss stood.

"Burgiss," Pelus warned.

Burgiss ignored him.

"Dorin," Burgiss asked, "did you hear anything last night?"

"Why would I have heard anything?" Dorin asked.

"You had night duty," Burgiss said.

"No, I didn't hear anything but the usual," Dorin said.

"Burgiss," Pelus said, "let it be."

"I think Braghin and Jaim are beating up my student at night," Burgiss said.

"Burgiss, it's okay," I tried to say.

"Stay out of this one, Kimi," Pelus warned.

"Marvus is the only one who's here for punching people," Dorin said.

"I don't think it's him," Burgiss said. "I don't know for certain. I can't speak to them, but you can at least speak to Braghin."

"And do you think your student is a perfect angel?" Dorin asked.

"They're all here to be retrained," Burgiss said. "Not to be punished by their own peers."

"You train your student your way," Dorin said. "I'll train my student in mine. I haven't had one fail yet."

Pelus made a sound.

"That's because you pick the safest ones," Burgiss said.

"None of them are safe, Burgiss," Dorin said. "Any of them can fail if you train them improperly."

"It's the worst-kept secret that that isn't true," Burgiss said.

"Burgiss," Pelus said, "if you want your student to have even a small chance of being retrained, you need to spend your time on lessons." I heard a pause. "Don't give me that look, Burgiss. You have a student to teach."

Burgiss grumbled something, moving away.

"If you taught them properly," Ossik spoke up, "maybe they wouldn't fail."

"Ossik," Dorin said, "leave it here. The point is made."

We made our way to the back room.

"Are you okay?" I asked Burgiss again.

"Yes, I'm fine," Burgiss said. "I'm sorry I was late. They were giving me more lessons for you to learn. Not sure how you can learn them when you're getting beaten up at night."

"It's fine," I said. "It really is."

"It's not fine," Burgiss said.

The door opened, and Pelus and Marvus came in.

"Burgiss," Pelus said, "I know as well as I do what day it is. You know it affects your judgment."

"I know," Burgiss said reluctantly.

"What day is it?" I asked.

"It's nothing," Burgiss said.

"Tell him, Burgiss," Pelus said gently.

"It's my friend's birthday," Burgiss said reluctantly.

"Uh..." I said.

"He's been gone a few years," Burgiss said. "I shouldn't be letting it get in the way, though. So, today's lesson."

"It's because you care so much about justice," Pelus said. "Somehow, you still do."

"Hm," Burgiss replied.

"What happened to your friend?" I asked.

"How much do you know about math?" Burgiss asked.

I blinked. "Um, I know math."

"Can you add and subtract?"

"Yeah."

"Multiply and divide?"

"Yeah, I can do that," I said.

"You probably don't know about shapes, though," Burgiss said. "Because you can't see."

"I know shapes," I said. "Circles, spheres..."

"Can you measure the degrees of a triangle?"

"Oh, yeah, I know that," I said. "So, you can't listen that accurately, but if you hear sound come back at you at about a 60 degree angle, then you know the ground sloped about 30 degrees before the wall. Or, if you hear sound reflect off a wall at a 120 degree angle, you know the ceiling slants about 60 degrees and you know where you have to duck."

"So, you know geometry!" Burgiss said. "What other math do you know?"

"Oh, lots of math," I said. "It's easy."

"You must know basic math and algebra then," Burgiss said.

"Oh yeah," I said. "Algebra's easy. You just have to pay attention to how the numbers dance from one side of the equation to the other."

Burgiss's face lit up. "How much geometry do you know? If you know angles, do you know how to calculate volume and area?"

"Easily!" I said. "We probably think about it differently, though, because you can hear how much area something takes. You can hear how big a diameter is, and how tall something is, and then you calculate from there."

"What about trigonometry?" Burgiss said.

"That's a little trickier," I said. "But it's easy once you understand sine and cosine. You know how sound moves? It moves like a wave, like this." I traced with my hand. "And then, when it reaches your ear, those waves are what make these tiny bones in your ear move. And that's how you hear. And if you can remember how sound moves, you can remember how sine and cosine work, and then it's pretty easy."

"That's amazing!" Burgiss said. "You could probably teach me a thing or two about math."

"Could teach me a fair amount too," Pelus mumbled.

"You just have to think about it like sound," I said. "Algebra's like a dance. Trigonometry is like music."

"Halmo always told me he saw art in calculus graphs," Burgiss said. "But that's why he's a scientist, and I'm..." He shrugged with a self-conscious laugh.

"Why you're what?" I asked, puzzled.

Burgiss hesitated. "Let's just say that there's not much prestige to teaching someone in the retraining program."

"To say the least," Pelus said.

"Was Halmo your friend?" I asked.

"He—oh, no," Burgiss said. "No, he's a friend of mine, but not the friend I was talking about. You should meet him. I'll be allowed to bring you out of here soon, just for the day. Most of the students will be doing career work, and you'll have to as well, but Halmo can teach you more than I can about, well, you're a much better student than I am, so Halmo can help you with math and science."

"The only thing they'll let him be is the likes of us," Pelus said.

"I'm still planning to go home," I said.

"Still?" Pelus asked.

"Yeah," I said. "I have to tell them not to go here. I don't get why no one else has gone back."

They were silent.

"Tell him, Burgiss," Pelus said.

"Not yet," Burgiss replied.

"Tell me what?" I asked.

Burgiss hesitated. "Uh... So, you know math. That puts you further ahead than I thought. And further ahead than they thought. So, let's work on more tricks for reading."

"I'm starting to figure out how your letters feel," I said. "They definitely feel different from ours, but it's starting to make sense."

"That's good," Burgiss said. "But you still need to learn how to see them a little if they test you. They might not press their pens into the paper enough to leave a mark."

I had trouble feeling even some of the letters that Burgiss had written.

"I'm sure they will forgive that you can't see well," Burgiss said.

"You know they won't, Burgiss," Pelus said.

"No, I know," Burgiss said. "But hopefully, by then...especially if you already know math."

"You'll need to teach him how to write it out too," Burgiss said.

Burgiss sighed. "Yeah, I have to teach that."

"Maybe I can help," Marvus said.

"No, you have your own lessons," Pelus said.

"To be more patient," Marvus said. "I know. And if I'm teaching Kimi, I have to be patient so that he can learn."

Pelus hesitated. "Alright."

Marvus, sweet though he was, struggled to teach me anything. I was still figuring out how to write even the most basic equations by midday, even though I could calculate everything in my head before I drew the first line. By the time it was time to set up for the midday meal, I still had learned nothing.

While Burgiss and I cleaned, I couldn't help overhearing Luchia.

"You must have something really wrong with you," Luchia was saying.

"No more than you," Marvus said back.

"The only friend you have is the weird kid," Luchia said. "And it's scientific fact that people get along with people who are like them."

"Maybe you should talk to him," Marvus said. "You'll like him too."

"Marvus, it's okay," I called to him.

"This doesn't have anything to do with you, Spy," Luchia said.

"Yeah, it does," I said.

"Living Light," Aika said. "What's with that kid? Always listening in and getting his nose into everything."

"Leave him alone," Marvus said.

"Marvus," Pelus cautioned.

"They're the ones picking on him," I said.

"This is the lesson he needs to learn, Kimi," Pelus said. "And you'd be wise to learn it too."

"Pelus—" Burgiss started.

"Don't start," Pelus said. "You're worse than the two of them together. I know there is no hope for you."

I heard the smile under Pelus's voice though. And I think Burgiss did too.

I realized only at the end of the day that Burgiss had never answered my question.

# 6

I'd seen the shadow-snatcher around six times by the time Dorin announced that we'd be able to leave occasionally with our mentors. "For career-training," Dorin said. "If you're successfully retrained, you will need to find a job."

I was looking forward to it. I knew this white box room by heart by now. I only wished that I could leave at night. Jaim's anxiety had made night a little easier, but I still raced to be in my bunk at night. If I was fast enough, I would only hear the boys announce my new nickname: Spy.

It was Burgiss's and my turn to clean up after morning meal. I noticed Dorin and Braghin had already left. They hadn't even waited for the meal to be finished.

"Hey, Spy," Jaim said. "You missed a spot."

"I'm still cleaning," I said.

"Well, you missed a spot," he said.

I tapped on the table, hoping a vibration would tell me what he meant. Nope, I had to look.

As soon as I saw, I knew I had not missed a spot. I would have noticed if a few half-eaten bones had been on the table still. From the smell, I knew they had come from the trash. Last night's meal, I thought.

I rolled my eyes, using a napkin to sweep them back into the trash.

I must have been zoned out, trying too hard to see, because I did not see Ossik until I crashed into him.

"Watch where you're going!" Ossik protested.

"I'm sorry," I said, backing up.

"You stupid boy!" Ossik scolded. "How long have you been retraining. A month? And you still can't—"

I heard Burgiss drop a bucket and winced at the clatter. I heard his footsteps.

"He can't help it, Ossik," Burgiss said. "He can't see."

"Your student is oblivious except where it suits him," Ossik said.

"He didn't see you," Burgiss said. "That is all."

"You know what the other students call him?" Ossik said. "Spy. Do you ever wonder why?"

"Because he can hear," Burgiss said. "That's all."

"If your student wasn't already doomed—" Ossik said.

"You do not have to make it harder for him," Burgiss said firmly.

"He might have a chance if his mentor wasn't useless," Ossik said.

Maybe I should have spoken, but in that moment I was too scared.

Burgiss scoffed. "Oh, I'm useless? Where is your student from last year? Is he still in prison?"

Ossik shoved him so hard that he stumbled.

I heard Pelus's feet.

"At least my students—" Ossik started.

Burgiss yelled something over him. I couldn't hear what either said. But I saw Ossik's fist, and I saw Burgiss's arm raise.

Pelus's palm clamped on Ossik's fist. His other hand clamped on Burgiss's shoulder.

"I am trying to teach my student not to use violence!" Pelus barked. "You are undermining that!"

I felt the depth of Pelus's voice reverberate through the room. When his voice fell silent, the silence felt alive.

"Burgiss, I'll speak with you to the side." Pelus's voice dropped back to a growl. "Ossik, keep your silence. I will speak to you after."

I was surprised when Ossik said nothing.

"Kimi," Pelus said, "keep cleaning. Marvus, help him."

I went back to mopping. I heard Marvus pick up the bucket.

Pelus and Burgiss went to the corner of the room. I tried not to listen in, but I could not help overhearing.

"Burgiss," Pelus was whispering, "you know not to provoke him."

"I couldn't help it," Burgiss said. "He was attacking my student!"

"You can't protect him from everything," Pelus said. "Let him fend for himself where he can, and let their comments slide. Their words don't matter anyway. Yours will matter more than anything else—to him and to the council."

Burgiss said nothing.

"Burgiss," Pelus said, "you might not be in retraining anymore, but you're still my student, and I don't want you getting yourself into more trouble than necessary."

"I can take it," Burgiss said.

"There are rumblings, Burgiss," Pelus said. "Yes, you are not in retraining, but there are other ways they can punish you if you step out of line."

Burgiss said nothing.

"Your student's about done," Pelus said. "I'll speak with Ossik after you leave."

There hadn't been much left. Marvus and I were just putting everything back into the broom closet.

Burgiss stepped away from Pelus silently.

"Kimi," Burgiss said, "are you ready?"

"Yeah," I said.

When the main door opened, a part of me could not quite believe we were stepping through. I felt my heart pick up speed and adrenaline run through my veins. When I stepped past that threshold, I filled with pure joy.

"Feels good to leave," Burgiss said, "doesn't it?"

"Yeah, it does," I agreed.

"It always does the first time," Burgiss said.

Burgiss took my hand.

It was strange to hear unfamiliar passageways again, strange and thrilling. They were all varying amounts of too bright, of course, but at least the soundscape finally changed.

"Kimi," Burgiss said, "don't try to listen for where you are. We don't have much time."

That was hard. I didn't trust my steps. I could hear them still, but I didn't have enough time to hear the echo before I had to step again.

Burgiss stopped, knocking on the wall before us.

"Halmo," Burgiss said, "it's us."

The door opened to a place where the Light seemed brightest of all.

I had to squint to see the man before us. He was younger than Burgiss, I thought. He had straight hair cut short, and I thought he had something on his eyes.

"Hi Burgiss," Halmo greeted. His voice was very soft. "And is this Kimi?"

"Yes," Burgiss said.

I smiled holding out a hand. "Nice to meet you. Burgiss has told me a lot about you."

Halmo hesitated before shaking my hand. "He's told me fathoms about you." He stepped back. "Come in."

Burgiss led me inside. Halmo shut the door.

I tapped to hear my surroundings. How bare this room was, as bare as every other place I'd seen so far. All I could hear was a bench beside us. I reached to brush it to be sure of where it was.

"It's very bright in here," I said.

"Yes," Halmo said. "Because this is where we work on the Light itself."

"Is that why you have things on your eyes?" I asked. "Do they protect your eyes?"

Halmo adjusted the item I'd seen. "No, these are just glasses. They help me to see better."

"Would glasses make me see better?" I asked Burgiss.

"No," he said. "His sight problems are different from yours."

"Burgiss said you were a scientist," I said to Halmo.

"I am," Halmo said. "I just finished my internship, and now I'm one of the main mechanics in charge of keeping the Light in repair."

Was I only imagining the strange undertone in his voice?

"Have you taught him about the mechanics of the Light yes?" Halmo asked.

Burgiss hesitated, looking down. "No, I haven't."

"Burgiss," Halmo said, "you have to teach him some time."

"I know," Burgiss sighed. "I don't want to."

"I know you don't," Halmo said, "but you're doing him no favors."

"I know," Burgiss said again.

"I can tell him," Halmo said, "if you want."

"No, I should tell him," Burgiss said.

"I can tell him," Halmo said again. "I know you will wait."

"That's not why I brought him here," Burgiss said. "I brought him here because you both understand math and science so differently from me, and I thought you'd both learn."

"You know better than anyone how my science is applied," Halmo said.

Burgiss was quiet again.

"What does he mean?" I asked Burgiss.

"I can tell him," Halmo said. "Better, maybe, to hear the bad news from someone else."

Burgiss said nothing.

"You can't hide it from him forever."

"I'll tell him tonight," Burgiss said. "If you talk about math and science, he'll learn more from you than me."

"Then I'll show him some of the mechanics," Halmo said. "I'm guessing you do not want to join us."

"I'd rather not," Burgiss said.

"Kimi, I can show you how the electromagnetic currents work."

"Uh...yeah, sure," I said. "What are they?"

"I'll explain where Burgiss isn't going to complain about it hurting his head."

"Ha, ha," Burgiss said flatly. "This place already gives me a headache with all of its Light."

"I know," Halmo said.

Halmo opened another door. I followed him, and the door closed.

"The tender-hearted fool," Halmo said sadly. "I think he wants you to learn everything you can before you learn the harshest truth about this place. He's too hopeful for his own good."

I blinked.

"Be very careful where you move here," Halmo cautioned. "A clumsy move can end your life."

I froze. "Then why did you bring me here?"

"Because I don't want Burgiss to hear," Halmo said. "Here, I'll take your hand, and I'll make sure you step only in safe places."

"I'll stay here if you don't mind," I said.

Halmo was quiet a moment. "Alright. I understand. I have not earned your trust yet. You're wise not to trust anyone here."

I inched closer to the door.

"This is one of the places where we work on the Light's mechanics," Halmo said. "We make sure its connections are working, that its safeguards are working, and that it's producing the right types of light in the right places. Light is not just what you see. Light is different colors, but it's also wavelengths you can't see. We need some of those wavelengths to survive, but more importantly, our plants need those wavelengths so that we have food."

"Your food needs light?" I asked.

"Yes," Halmo said. "We grow food that depends on

light. Our water-cleaning system depends on different types of light. Our waste treatment uses light. Everything—everything—depends on light in some way. And that light is mostly electricity."

"Which is?" I asked.

Halmo paused. "So...you know how sometimes you rub cloth and you get a snap and a spark of light?"

"Yeah," I said.

"It's like that."

"Okay," I said. "I think I get it."

Halmo was quiet.

"So," I said, "what else?"

"This is useless," Halmo said.

"What?" I asked.

"I can't explain the Light without explaining everything," Halmo said. "Kimi, do not misunderstand. Burgiss has your best interests in mind, and he cares very deeply for his students. But you need to know what the Light is."

I could hear my heartbeat in my ears.

"Kimi," Halmo said, "to understand the Light, you have to understand where we come from. I don't know if you have a similar story, but we used to live on the surface."

"Really?" I asked.

"It was not always so hostile as it is now," Halmo said. "Back then, the surface was a safe place. There were rocky cliffsides to shelter us. We've preserved ancient art and stories that describe how the surface used to be. Less well preserved are the stories of how things changed. Why the storms became so intense, the air so thick, the temperature so hot, or so cold, that it drove us underground.

"We came here used to constant, or near-constant, light. We'd never known absolute darkness. We didn't know how to survive without it, how to grow the food we'd always had, or even how to understand our surroundings. So, we created a machine that created light."

"And that's the Light," I said.

"No," Halmo said. "That was the first of the Light's predecessors. We started with a light that depended on burning fuel. We started with fuels from the surface that we gathered at great risk. Many people lost their lives obtaining this fuel. But the fuel sources we knew from the surface died, or they ran out. I'm not sure which.

"So, we changed our fuel source. We found minerals underground that created fuel, in one way or another. Some we burned. Some we turned into batteries. It was the batteries that gave us some way to sustain the light, but only if we had the fuel to supplement them, or restore them. And it wasn't enough. The rock-born fuels we used ran out, and we had to move farther and farther away from the Light to find them. People began to get lost seeking the fuel, or lose their breath in places where there was no oxygen to breathe.

"Out of desperation, we created the Light that we have today. It runs on batteries, like the previous machine, but it still needs energy to maintain it." Halmo looked grave. "This Light depends on living cells. Every year, it needs a large enough life form so it can sustain itself on the energy of that life form's living cells after the being is gone, preferably ones that regenerate quickly so that their growth temporarily outpaces how quickly they are consumed."

Something in my stomach turned.

"And the life form is..." I said.

"Humans, Kimi," Halmo said. "They're the only life form we have here that is big enough. One human can sustain the Light for a full year. And usually, it's a teenager or a young adult because they're large enough to sustain the Light, and their cells are still repairing and regenerating fast enough."

I stared.

"Every year," Halmo continued, "the counsel selects a few troubled youths who have been going against their society, who've gotten into serious trouble, or gotten into trouble too many times. These youths are put into a retraining program to see if they can learn to be part of our society. The one who does most poorly is sacrificed to the Light to sustain the rest of us."

My stomach dropped.

"And that's what..." I trailed off.

"Yes," Halmo said.

I swallowed. "So one of us is going to be..." I almost couldn't get the words out. "They're going to kill one of us."

"Yes," Halmo said again. "It's the only way to sustain the Light."

"Okay. So, oh—" I caught myself before I could swear, swallowing it back. "So, I have to learn how to be like you or they'll throw me into the Light?"

"Kimi," Halmo said. He hesitated. "This year is a sham, and you're the only one who didn't know. They know you have no idea how this place works. They know you can't see, and they know that you can never understand how to operate in the Light when you haven't needed it for fifteen years. They are all expecting that you will fail."

I took a step toward him. "If this is some sick joke—"

"Kimi," Halmo interrupted, raising a cautioning hand. He lowered it. "It's no joke. Burgiss did not want you to know, but it is not fair to keep you in the...the dark."

I drew back, bumping into the door.

"So you're all just teaching me this stuff as a game?" I spat. "Just to entertain you for a year?"

"No, Kimi," Halmo said. "Burgiss wants you to succeed, and he is working as hard as he can to give you a fighting chance."

"What for?" I demanded. "If they've already decided, what's the point?"

"Burgiss doesn't give up easily, Kimi," Halmo said. "I've seen him shatter himself trying to do the impossible, more than once. He's very fond of you Kimi, even knowing what will probably happen."

I wanted to punch something, or scream out. Preferably both. It took every ounce of willpower not to do either.

"I want to help you, Kimi," Halmo said. "You're bright. You're thoughtful. You're not the first person to so clearly not need retraining, but you stand a better chance than any of them because you learn so readily."

"And what good does that do?" I snapped. "Okay, so, by some miracle, maybe I'll be lucky and not be sacrificed to the Light. And then what? Someone else gets thrown into the Light instead?"

Halmo said nothing.

My fists clenched. "I have to talk to Burgiss about this."

"You should," Halmo agreed. "Hear what he has to say."

As if I wanted to know what Burgiss thought of raising me up like a gamefowl.

"Don't move," Halmo said. "Let me get the door."

"So it doesn't eat me too early?" I asked darkly.

"I can't argue," Halmo said sadly.

"Does it never eat mechanics?" I asked.

"Why do you think I was just promoted?" Halmo asked.

I flinched.

"Let me know when you're ready," Halmo said.

I couldn't think how to approach Burgiss. How angry did I want to be with him? Very, I thought. But I needed enough control to express it right. Right now I was too angry to speak.

I waited, taking a few deep breaths, fists clenched.

"Okay," I said.

He opened the door.

# 7

I felt my preparations fall away as the door opened. Still, I stepped forward. I heard the door close.

Burgiss looked up at me. He braced.

"You know what I'm about to ask you," I said.

"I know," Burgiss said.

"So," I said, "that's why you're retraining me."

"That's why I'm supposed to retrain you," Burgiss said flatly.

"When were you going to tell me?" I demanded.

Burgiss said nothing.

"Were you just going to let me sleepwalk to being sacrificed?" I yelled at him.

"No," Burgiss choked. He shrank back as if he'd been punched in the stomach.

I was too angry to be sympathetic.

"When were you going to tell me?" I asked, more winded this time.

Burgiss swallowed. I waited.

"Kimi," Burgiss said, "I'm not so far past nearly..." He sank down, trembling.

I blinked, sitting next to him.

"Some of us were retrained longer ago than others," Burgiss said, "but none of us have forgotten what it is like to be in your place."

It occurred to me only then that Burgiss was younger than I thought.

"How old are you?" I asked.

"Eighteen," Burgiss said.

My eyes bulged.

Burgiss smiled self-consciously. "I look older than I am."

"Uh, yeah," I said awkwardly. "I mean, sorry. I mean—"

"No, you're right," Burgiss said. "And it's...it's not going to happen to you, but the last part of my retraining took a lot out of me."

"When were you retrained?" I asked.

"Three years ago," Burgiss said.

"That's it?" I asked.

"That's it," Burgiss said.

"You don't seem like someone who would have to be retrained," I said.

Burgiss laughed, and I heard the pain behind it. "Kimi, if you'd known me three years ago, you wouldn't say that."

I waited.

"So?" I said. "Tell me."

Burgiss took a deep breath.

"I come from a shadowed past, Kimi," Burgiss said. "The men in my life were violent, and in some cases criminal, and I thought that was what I had to be. I had no other role models. It's not what I wanted to become, but I thought I had no other choice. So, I spent time with the wrong sort. I got into trouble more than a few times for small things. Even so, I was bad at...I didn't like thinking I'd hurt someone, so I fell short every time of who I thought I was supposed to be. I thought I was barely a boy, much less a man. But because of that, I chose poor company. Because I hated doing dangerous or harmful things, I did them poorly, and I was always caught when I failed. So, I became known for being deeply shadowed.

"One day, I was with a few friends. Well, I use the term loosely. Knowing what I know now, they weren't my friends. One day, I was with them. They drew a bunch of graffiti. I think I drew some too. And then, while I was drawing, they stole a few of the cables we use to carry the Light. It was fool-hardy. It could have killed them if they'd done it wrong. I didn't steal anything, but I was too stupid to run when they did. Why would I run? I didn't do the stealing."

I said nothing.

"That's when I was put into the retraining program," Burgiss said, "the same one you're in now. I was not a good student, Kimi. Not like you. I was stupid and stubborn. Pelus did his best, but half of the time I didn't understand because what he was teaching me was so different from what I'd learned. I would have been the sacrifice. Should have been. I would have been if one other kid wasn't just as stupid and stubborn as me." He swallowed. "We knew better, but we became fast friends, then best friends. He taught me more than my own teacher did. And I think we pretended that we didn't know what was coming.

"But the day came, and they could not decide which of us had done more poorly, which of us remained most shadowed. So they put us both through grueling trials. Some of it was laborious, some strenuous, some knowledge-based, some learning-based. We were pitted against each other. When one of us started to fall back, though, the other would purposefully stall, so we remained evenly matched. But he gave up first. I stalled to try to give him a chance, but by then, we were both spent. I don't even remember what happened from there, only that three days later, I knew he was gone."

I didn't know what to say. I knew I had to say something, so I opened my mouth. I swore.

Burgiss nodded.

"I guess that's the shadow I'll admit this time," I mumbled.

Burgiss laughed breathlessly.

"Burgiss, that's awful," I said. "And I'm really sorry you went through that."

Burgiss shrugged. "It's...I know they need one person to keep the Light going. I never see anyone who deserves it. But you deserve it even less than everyone else. You don't need the Light. By now I'm sure you don't even want the Light."

"Not anymore, I don't," I said.

"I want you to have a fighting chance," Burgiss said. "It might be in vain, and you should know that. But you're doing so well, at least you can force them to have to explain. You're not like me. You aren't shadowed. Your only fault is that you're foreign and you can't see well."

"Yeah, that will be enough for them," I said.

Burgiss pursed his lips.

"It gets a little harder each year," Burgiss said. "The ceremony, but everything else too. When you're here, you think, okay, your goal is not to fail, even if you know it will probably be you. But then the next year, once I was recovered enough to think, you know it before but that's when you realize that this happens every year to a new group, and every year there's going to be one person that fails. I tried to find work that year, but my reputation followed me. Once you are retrained, even if you succeed, no one forgets it. But also, once you've been in retraining, once you know the cost of the Light, you just see the insidiousness of the Light in everything. Everything you do feeds into it. So, I came back. And now, each year, the new students look a little younger, a little more lost, a little more innocent, even knowing what some of them did. There are ways to retrain someone, but this is not it."

"You were angry at Dorin for taking easy students," I said.

Burgiss sighed angrily. "He and Ossik always choose someone who cannot fail. It makes them look good if their student succeeds, but it doesn't matter because they were going to anyway. But Ossik's student last year, you might have heard me say it, he didn't change. Ossik did him no favors because Ossik didn't teach him anything. He was arrested days after his release. I—Pelus and I, we choose the ones who don't deserve to be there, or the people who have the chance to learn, but our students are usually the ones chosen. It's the unfairness that makes me so angry."

"What happened to your other students?" I asked.

Burgiss was quiet a moment. "I think you know, Kimi. You heard Pelus say I was the guardian of lost causes. Both of my students failed. My first student, I don't know if I could have done something different or if he would have failed no matter what. My head says one thing, my heart another. My student last year, I couldn't get through to him. He gave up before he arrived." He swallowed. "I hate to think that this...this light is all that's left of him. And my previous student, not even that."

The thought made my skin crawl. With that new thought, the light seemed to burn my eyes a little more, and the heat felt unsettling.

"And everyone is okay with this?" I said. "Just knowing someone is going to be sacrificed every year?"

"No one is," Burgiss said. "They think of it as a necessary evil. But I think the price of the Light is far greater than the one young life we sacrifice per year." His hands clenched tightly. "I hate everything about it. I just wish it would...I don't know. I wish the darkness we're so scared of would claim it even if it takes us with it." He paused. "At least, I did until I met you. You always managed without the Light. Maybe we can too."

"Didn't you choose me because I was destined to fail?" I asked, more bitterly than intended.

"No, I didn't," Burgiss said. "I gravitate toward those students because I was one of them myself. When I saw you, you looked so lost. Because you were. You had no idea what was going on. But you also seemed so unshakably hopeful. This is not a place of hope, Kimi, and to see hope for the first time in so long, that's what made me want to teach you. But that's also why I could not figure out how to tell you."

I was not fully ready to forgive him yet.

"If you really think it's not okay," I said, "you could help me get out of here."

"No, I couldn't," Burgiss said.

"Why not?" I asked.

"Because I don't know a way out," Burgiss said. "There are almost no ways to leave, and almost no one is allowed to leave. And especially those of us who were in retraining. Halmo's the only person I know who's allowed to leave. He told me once that there are special exits that the mechanics use."

"But are there ways out?" I asked.

"Very few," Burgiss said, "and they are all closely guarded. I'm impressed you found a way in."

"Well, maybe that way is still open," I said. "You can bring me there."

"No, they already sealed it over," Burgiss said. "Shortly after the ceremony."

I swallowed back another curse.

The door opened, and Halmo stepped in.

Burgiss looked up. "Halmo, I said I was going to tell him tonight."

"You were not going to tell him, Burgiss," Halmo said. "I know you. I know you had every intention of telling him tonight, but something was going to get in the way, somehow."

"Still," Burgiss said, "I should have been the one to tell him."

Halmo had no response.

Burgiss was quiet a moment. "We're almost out of time. We should go back before we are missed."

None of us could bring ourselves to give a word of farewell.

We were silent all of the way back. I only faintly recognized our path back. When we entered, everyone else was already back. I was still trying to process what I had just learned.

"Kimi?" Marvus asked. "Are you alright?"

"Yeah," I lied. "Yeah, I'm fine."

I heard the flatness of my voice, but Marvus did not press.

During dinner, everyone was talkative. They were all talking about what they had done on their day out. Burgiss and I were silent. I only nudged at my food, not able to bring myself to eat. Burgiss's head was low.

"You told him?" Pelus whispered.

"Halmo told him," Burgiss whispered back.

"Kimi," Marvus asked, "what did you do?"

I shrugged. "I, uh, not much. Um, I learned a bit about electronics. You?"

"Pelus brought me to see my family," Marvus said. "Are you sure you're okay?"

"Yeah, I'm fine," I said.

But I knew Marvus wasn't convinced. I could barely bring myself to speak. When I climbed into my bunk, I almost could not sleep.

—

What a strange dream I had that night.

I dreamed that I was part of the Light. At least, that's what it was in the dream. The Light was bright everywhere, with nothing resembling a shadow anywhere, but the sounds of the Light were my home cave, all of the way to that familiar bulge in the ceiling where you had to duck. I was surrounded by people, some familiar and some not. Burgiss was there, and Marvus, and Pelus. But all of us glowed white, and one person kept turning into some sort of bat with a duck bill. I knew in the dream that our unspoken purpose was to save people from the darkness.

So, I left. For some reason, I hovered, making no sound, but even so, I could hear in the tiniest echoes where I was going.

And then I found someone, and I knew from their footsteps that they were lost in the dark.

I went to them.

"Are you okay?" I asked.

"I can't see," the person said.

"Neither can I," I said.

"Yes," the person said. "But I need to see. I need light."

And I thought. I could bring this person to the Light. Everything told me I should. But I already knew that as soon as I brought this person to the Light, that person would depend on me—on us—forever.

I knew what to do. It wasn't exactly what I was supposed to do, but I knew in my heart what was right.

"This is how you make light," I told them.

As if from nowhere, I was able to conjure these candles we sometimes used if we were going to a new tunnel that might not be safe. But they were long, almost as long as my forearm.

I set it down, and with a tiny mechanism made from flint and steel, I lit a spark. The candle burned.

As if in a trance, I conjured another candle, setting it down, and lighting it. And another, each time in an identical set of motions, as if my mind was looping the same thought over and over. When I finished, there were six candles, all in a circle around the person.

"Keep them all burning," I said, handing them the flint and steel, "and you will always have your light."

The person was still staring in amazement at the light that surrounded them. I smiled, and I left.

I was proud of myself. The person had their Light, and we would not have to help them again because now they would always be able to help themselves.

But when I returned to the place where I had lived in the Light, there was a boulder across it. No, a door. A stone door that fit over the cave entrance. The world was black.

I was confused, then angry. This was where the Light was supposed to be, and I had done the right thing. There was no reason I could not go in.

I held a sword. I was not sure how I'd gotten a sword. I slashed it, and the door gashed open as if made of paper. It was dark on the other side.

As if disembodied, I watched myself climb through the slash in the door. But as I climbed through, I somehow accidentally climbed straight through to an identical slash through the back of the cave, and I fell somewhere behind it into blackness.

And in that blackness, I understood. The Light was not real. It had never been real, not even in my memory.

# 8

Back home, they always said that I would find a reason to smile even if the sky crashed into the caverns. Now I knew they were wrong.

I didn't want to look at anyone. I didn't feel like talking. I sat silently through another meal, barely eating. Burgiss was no better.

When we went to the side room, I didn't even want to look at Burgiss. I didn't want to be anywhere near him.

"Kimi," Burgiss said, "I know you don't feel like it, but we still need to do your lessons."

I said nothing.

Burgiss put a paper in my hands. I ignored it.

"Kimi," Burgiss said gently, "you still need to learn how to write."

I said nothing.

"Here," Burgiss coaxed. "At least show me how you hold the pen."

I did not move.

"Kimi," Burgiss pleaded. "Don't give up. It's not about them. But if you give up, then it is."

I said nothing.

"They're all like this when they first arrive," Pelus said. "You were, on your first days. He's in his first days, a few months late."

Burgiss said nothing.

"Let me try speaking to him," Pelus said. "You can mentor my student for the morning."

"Are you sure?" Burgiss asked.

"I'm sure," Pelus said. "Marvus needs to hear someone other than an old curmudgeon anyway."

Burgiss looked up. "Marvus, are you alright with that?"

"I—" Marvus shrugged. "I mean, I do not mind listening to Pelus, but it might be helpful to learn from you. To get another perspective."

"Alright," Burgiss said.

They both stood, and they both left. I heard the door close.

"It does you no good to be angry, kid," Pelus said.

I said nothing.

"Because you cannot control who your anger affects," Pelus said. "It affects the people around you and never the object of your anger."

I shrugged.

"I know you are angry at Burgiss," Pelus said. "But—"

"I'm not," I interrupted.

"Really?" Pelus asked. "It sure seems it. You sling your anger at him with the weight of a rockfall."

"No, I'm not angry at him." I paused. "Well, maybe a little. I understand why he didn't tell me. But still, he should have."

"He should have," Pelus said. "But it was not just Burgiss. No one told you. Not even the boys who beat you up every night."

I blinked.

"It's an unwritten rule that we do not talk about it," Pelus said. "We don't tell children. It's something they find out, or they are told as teenagers. Here, we do not talk about it because it will be one of you, and even when it seems certain who it is, it is not guaranteed."

"It seems guaranteed this year," I said.

"It does," Pelus said. "But a few years ago, it was guaranteed to be Burgiss."

"They're not likely to change their minds this year," I said.

"No," Pelus agreed. "They are not."

We were quiet a moment.

"How do you know who it's going to be?" I asked.

"You hear people talk," Pelus said. "You learn the patterns. Some of them, they were never going to be chosen. They almost never choose a girl. I only saw it happen once."

"Is that why Luchia and Aika's mentors are never here?" I asked.

Pelus smiled wryly. It was weird seeing Pelus smile. It was frightening seeing the anger behind it.

"Yes, that's why," he said. "Because they know it's not going to be a girl. It's because most people out there mistakenly think girls are more innocent than boys, so it looks bad if the council chooses a girl. And it was never going to be Braghin. His mother's on the council. He's only here because he's caused so much damage that it would look bad if he wasn't put into retraining. He's vandalized half our structures, beaten up any kid he wants, and in general treated everything and everyone with contempt. But everyone knows this is just to scare some sense into him. Jaim's a thief, but he is also from a well-to-do background." He paused. "But Marvus is from a hard-luck family. I retrained his uncle long ago. This year, it was no secret that Marvus was chosen to fail."

"You taught Marvus's uncle?" I asked.

"I did," Pelus said.

"Did he make it?" I asked.

"No," Pelus said. "Marvus never met him."

I swallowed.

"How long have you been a teacher?" I asked.

"I've been retraining students for twenty years," Pelus said. "And every year, it's the same. The students come in. You retrain them. Some cannot fail. One always will. You watch the ceremony. You go back to the same retraining room, and there is a new year of students waiting. I'm tired of the same pattern. But being angry will not change that."

"Have you thought of doing something else?" I asked. "If you're tired of it?"

"After twenty years," Pelus said, "there is not much else I am qualified to do. After you are retrained, even if you succeed, the reputation follows you, and there are few jobs you are allowed to do. And when you've taught for so long, there's little convincing someone that you can do something else."

I had no response.

"It's almost time to start preparing the midday meal," Pelus said. "You should go."

I stood. At the door, I paused.

"Thank you, Pelus," I said. "And good luck."

"You need the luck more, kid," Pelus said.

I still wasn't ready to speak to Burgiss yet as we cooked. I still was quiet through the meal. But as I ate, I thought. I thought back to a cave I had seen before. I had gone there many times with my family. It was filled with glowworms. I missed that place.

As we went back, I finally turned to Burgiss.

"What does Halmo think of the Light?" I asked.

"I don't know," Burgiss said. "I think probably the same as everyone else: that it's a necessary evil."

"Could we see Halmo again?" I asked.

Burgiss looked surprised. "You want to go back there?"

"Yes," I said.

"I can see if I can arrange for it," Burgiss said, "but it will take a few days."

"That's okay," I said.

It did take a few days, and in the meantime, Burgiss tried tirelessly to teach me lessons that I could not possibly learn.

"Kimi," Burgiss said, "that's not the correct way to hold a pen. You have to hold it like this. No, that letter is not shaped right. No, that is supposed to be a curve. Here, feel the way this letter is shaped and now feel this one. Do you feel the difference?"

I couldn't help it. It was so ridiculous. I smiled. And I laughed.

"I missed hearing that sound," Burgiss said.

"I'm not going to figure this out," I said.

"Yes, you will," Burgiss said. "Here, feel here. You can almost write your name. It's only the one letter that's giving you trouble now."

"Yeah, I'm going to have to be able to write more than my name," I said.

"And you'll get there," Burgiss said.

"Even though I can't see?" I asked.

"You're learning by feel," Burgiss said, "and you are almost there. And it gives us something to work on. Just imagine how foolish the council will look if you can write."

"And if I figure it out?" I asked.

"Then we wait while the council twists themselves backwards to figure out another lesson for you."

I smiled. This time, I smiled without anger. At least, not anger toward Burgiss.

A few days later, we made our way to Halmo's place. I distantly recognized the path. I recognized the door, and I recognized the sound of Burgiss knocking.

The door opened, and I recognized the flood of light.

"You really wanted to come back?" Halmo asked, surprised.

"Yes," I said.

"Did you want to come in?" he asked.

"I'd rather not," Burgiss said.

"I know you wouldn't," Halmo said.

I entered, and Halmo closed the door.

"Why did you want to come back?" Halmo asked.

"I wanted to talk more about the Light," I said, "and what you do."

"I'm surprised you want to know anything more," Halmo said.

"How many coworkers do you have?" I asked.

"That's a very specific question," Halmo said suspiciously.

"What I mean is," I said, "how many people work on the Light? Or, what do they think of the Light?"

"There's not much to be thought about it," Halmo said.

"Okay, this might sound crazy," I said, "but what if you could change the Light so no one would have to be sacrificed to it?"

"We can't replace the Light, Kimi," Halmo said, "and we can't convince them. They're frightened. They don't know how to live without the Light." Halmo's mouth slipped to a grim line. "Besides, there are people who derive their power from the Light, and they will not give it up easily."

"And if you could?" I asked.

"We can't, Kimi," Halmo said.

"Listen, I know it sounds crazy," I said, "but have you heard of glowworms?"

"I've heard of them," Halmo said.

"Have you seen them?" I asked.

"I haven't seen many," he replied.

"Listen, there's a cave full of them," I said, "and I could show you."

"There's no way to get out of here, Kimi," Halmo said.

"Burgiss said you know of a way out," I said.

"Of course he did," Halmo said. "Why can't Burgiss keep his big mouth shut for once?" He shook his head. "Listen, I can't let you out."

"Surely it's okay if it's under your supervision," I said.

"Even if it was," Halmo said, "no, I can't. If you ran, Burgiss and I would get into serious trouble. You know that."

"I wouldn't run," I said. "And even if I did, it's not like you'd be thrown to the Light."

"We probably would," Halmo said. "It's not just the one person per year. Once in a while, if someone commits a particularly unspeakable crime, they might be 'thrown to the Light' as you put it. And letting you escape would put us in that realm."

I blinked. "Wow. I didn't know that."

"You know very little," Halmo said.

"Uh..." I said. "Well, let's not talk about that yet. What would you think if you could replace the Light with something else?"

"It doesn't matter," Halmo said. "I can't convince them to change the Light."

"You don't like the Light, right?"

"No one likes it," Halmo said.

"So, who would you have to convince?" I asked. "Your coworkers?

"My coworkers would barely notice a difference," he said. "Mostly they're just making sure the wires work properly. The problem is the council."

"Why would you have to convince the council?" I asked.

"Because they are the ones who approve any changes to the Light," he said. "And that's almost impossible."

"How do you know?" I asked. "Have you tried?"

"I did," Halmo said. "A few years ago, I did some calculations, and I found ways to increase the energy efficiency of the Light so much that it would only need one person every two years, or even a smaller creature each year instead. I presented it to the council, but they wouldn't hear it. I learned later that five people before me had presented the same thing."

I felt my eyes grow wide. "Why wouldn't they—"

"As I said, they derive power from it. It's an instrument of fear to make sure people act right. If they step out of line, they're afraid they'll be used to fuel the Light, or their children will."

I was quiet.

"Well," I said, "what if you could change it without the council knowing?"

Halmo flinched. "That would be dangerous. If the council found out, at best they would fire me and sabotage my work. At worst, I'd be executed as well."

"I'm not going to ask you to do that," I said, "but listen, it's something to at least think about. Just thinking if there's a way to change this theoretically. And if there was another source of light, that would do it."

"Glowworms won't be enough, Kimi," Halmo said. "Even if theoretically we could find, grow, or breed enough glowworms to replace the visible light, it would only cover the blue spectrum. We'd need the other spectrums of visible light to avoid having people find out. And the Light also covers infrared and ultraviolet frequencies, and glowworms are not going to replace that."

"Well, maybe we don't have to think that far yet," I said. "We'll start with glowworms. It's a baby step. It's at least worth thinking about, right?"

Halmo said nothing.

"Let's pretend for a moment," I said, "we have the glowworms. We have your improvements. We find everything we need to change the Light, and no one has a problem with it. If you had nothing stopping you, could you replace the Light?"

Halmo hesitated. "If I could...I could slowly replace the Light over time, but it wouldn't be on time for you."

"I know," I said. "But would it be on time for the next person?"

Halmo paused, and he spoke too quietly. "For the next person, yes." He was quiet another moment. "How far away is the cave?"

"Not far," I said. "About fifteen minutes on foot."

"There is one exit where they will not see us. It is in the inner workings of the Light, and I'd have to lead you there to get there safely. It's an old emergency exit, and I'm not sure if it still works, but it's worth a try."

"Okay," I said. "You want to try it?"

"We'll try it," Halmo said. "You're lucky I think so highly of Burgiss and implicitly trust his assessment of you. I'm risking both of our lives for this excursion."

He reached by the door, grabbing something. He cranked a handle, and it whirred.

"What is that?" I asked.

"An emergency light," he said. "In case we have to work on a piece where the Light has failed. It will last an hour. I will keep track of time, and if we take more than fifteen minutes to get there, I will turn us both back. Understood?"

"Understood," I said.

He opened the door, closing it tightly after I stepped through. He took my hand.

Being back here a second time, especially now that I knew more about this place, was worse than the first time. It was too bright here. Danger was somewhere there, too close, but I couldn't hear where it was. Was it that buzzing around me?

I hate knowing this light is all that's left of him.

I felt my stomach turn.

"Are you alright?" Halmo asked.

"Yeah," I said.

He stopped. When I tapped, I thought I heard a place where the wall was shaped differently, but it was hard to tell through the buzzing.

"Here goes," Halmo said, dropping my hand. "Stay back Kimi."

He rammed himself into the oddly shaped piece of wall. I could hear now that it was a door. I heard it judder. He shoved again, and the door creaked. Halmo grunted and threw his weight against it.

The door moved with a protesting whine.

Halmo leaned against the doorframe, catching his breath, his arm blocking the exit.

I could see his shape. I moved a little closer to see better. Out there, there was darkness. Beautiful, welcome darkness. My eyes felt strange seeing it, but my heart ached for joy.

Halmo stood, taking my hand. We stepped out.

## 9

It wasn't until we stepped away that I realized how different it was out here. How silent it was without that constant background buzzing. My ears felt as if shackles had been removed from them. My eyes relished the softer light.

Softer, but not gone, because of Halmo's light.

"Give me one second," I said.

I listened. I tapped. I oriented myself, and I set off.

Halmo was nervous. I could tell because his steps were more shuffled, and he held my hand tighter.

"No running," Halmo said.

"I won't," I said. "But can we move a little faster?"

"I can't see well enough to move faster," Halmo said.

"It's okay," I said. "I can lead you. You led me through the bright light."

Halmo hesitated. "I'm not ready for that."

"Alright."

I speak as if we were moving slowly, but we weren't really. Halmo kept a normal pace. My legs were relieved to move a little faster in an area that was starting to sound familiar. Sound carried so much better when there wasn't more sound all around to muffle its echoes.

I could hear the angles of the world around me, sharply outlined. How fuzzy the world had seemed before. And now, it was defined, with subtle differences here and there. I could hear where the walls bulged or bent, where the floor was uneven or a stalactite might get under foot. I could hear where to duck, where to lean, and where to avoid.

I could feel myself smiling. This, I thought, was reason to smile again.

All that would make it better, I thought, was if I was not wearing shoes. Then I could feel the stone under my feet, and my echoes would sound familiar.

"How much further?" Halmo asked.

"We haven't gotten past the Light's area yet," I said.

"How much further from here?" Halmo asked.

"Don't worry, Halmo," I eased. "We're going down this big cavern. There's plenty of space, and the ground's stable here. You could probably burst into a blind run and not catch your feet on anything."

Halmo held my hand tighter.

"Could you loosen your hand a little?" I asked. "I'm losing circulation."

Halmo loosened his hold the barest amount.

I didn't navigate by echo so much as muscle memory. After so long, I'd been so worried that I would forget where I was. But no, every corner of this place was so familiar I remembered it by heart. I knew where the cavern turned away, where we had to slide through a narrow piece.

"We're almost there now," I said.

"It's been..." Halmo paused. "Only seven minutes?"

"Yeah, it's not far," I said. "And from here..."

I stopped. This place should have been familiar. But from here, the glowworm cave was not as familiar as the rest of the caverns. I'd been here many times, but those times, this place had been fully dark.

"It's weird being here and having so much light," I said.

"I'm sure," Halmo said.

I took a few steps. But with light, this place was so unfamiliar.

"I..." I paused. "Hold on, I'm really disoriented with the light."

"I'm not going to turn it off," Halmo said firmly.

"Oh, no, of course not," I said. "I...oh, hold on."

I closed my eyes.

It was still different. The intensity of the light, frail though it was in comparison to the Light, still lit my eyelids up in deep red.

I took a loud step, and I immediately felt disoriented. I heard my step, but the way it bounced, I couldn't catch anything. The sound seemed to fall erratically to my ear.

For a moment, my heart leapt to my throat. Had I forgotten this simple, bread-and-butter skill that had been second nature to me since before my infant mind could hold onto any other memory? Had I only imagined how clearly I'd heard before?

Or was it because I was wearing shoes? My shoes echoed differently. And how strange to not feel the floor with my foot. Had I been feeling the vibrations through my foot even more than I realized?

I heard my breath come in sharper and faster than usual. And although I didn't hear the echo clearly, it was there. It was the type of quiet echo you felt more than you heard.

The silence felt precious here, and the quiet vision. Slowly, I heard my ears begin that faint high-pitched buzzing they conjured only when they found no other sound, and when I took notice, the already-sharp note raised higher to a needle-point pitch. This sound that had once annoyed me so much, now I greeted it with a surge of joy. And slowly, my ears found that faint low rushing it always found second.

"Kimi—" Halmo said.

"Shh," I whispered. "I'm orienting myself."

And now I could feel the echoes of my whispers.

I stepped, I cocked my head and then I stamped.

The stamp rang just enough. I heard the split second echo, the way it bounced off the walls next to me. The echo came from the sides, from above and below, but not before and not behind.

And to my right, finally, I heard a familiar feature, a particular bulge in the wall that made the echo to my right a little louder, a little warped.

"I know where we are," I said, perhaps a little too loud. "Follow me!"

Halmo was so startled that his grip loosened. My hand was free before I realized.

I set off running, and I heard Halmo behind me. In my steps, I heard the echo along the ground and the places where it ended. I heard the familiar turn. I heard the sudden sharp end of the echo near a raised place and slowed down.

"Careful here," I said.

I said it loudly so that the echo would tell me that the floor existed past the raised bump. I stepped over and kept going.

"How do you do that?" Halmo asked.

"I'll show you later," I said. "There's a good spot near the glowworms."

"Careful!" Halmo warned.

I'd already heard it, the place where the ground dropped sharply to the side. I could hear in my step where the hard floor ended, but in our voices I heard the void there, and I heard the quiet echo within, too quiet and cavernous and too far below to be safe. But it was far less deep than Halmo seemed to think. I wondered if he saw less with his light than I heard with my echoes.

And then I heard the faint trickling water, and I knew we were almost there.

"Okay, hold on," I said. "I'll wait until you catch up."

Halmo came to me with timid footsteps, quiet but clear. I took his hand again. I stepped, and I went past the corner.

It did not matter how many times I saw this place. Every time, my wonder was recaptured. Before me spread shallow water, and the sound echoed strongly against this, perhaps a little louder than against the stone. Every time water dripped from above, it echoed in crystalline sounds. But above, sound was softened slightly by the glowworms' bodies, and in their place, a beautiful scattered glowing spread. Blue sparkles filled the cavern, long blue threads dangling down. Nothing, I thought, could ever match the beauty of this place.

I heard Halmo take a breath.

"Nice, isn't it?" I whispered.

"I've never seen so many in my life," he breathed.

"We're not far away," I said. "Not really."

"No," Halmo said.

"There are green ones too," I said. "So there's some color difference."

"Not enough," Halmo said, "but..."

I heard a step. Halmo did too. He was learning, I thought.

There was another step. A little closer this time. I saw the shape of a person.

"Kimi?" the man asked.

I recognized his voice before I recognized the sound of his long, leggy figure, the way the sound swept over the shape of his broad-jawed face.

"Iska!" I greeted.

I all but launched myself at him, embracing him. He embraced me back, and we were laughing, laughing loud.

"What is this, Kimi?" Iska said once he let me go. "What are these strange clothes? You seem good! You seem healthy."

I forced a smile. "Yeah, I am. You seem it too."

"Yeah, I'm good," Iska said. "Kimi, I didn't think you'd ever come back!"

I felt my face fall.

"Kimi?" Iska asked.

"He can't go back with you," Halmo said.

Iska's face fell too.

"Listen, it's complicated," I said. "But...Iska, it's not worth it to go there. Once you're there, you can't leave."

"Why not?" Iska asked. "You did."

"Only for a short time," I said.

But the thought came to me again. I could run. Right now, I could run. The two of us would be gone before Halmo could catch us.

But I remembered what Halmo had said. What could happen to Halmo and Burgiss. I couldn't bear that on my conscience.

Even in that moment, I knew the thought was foolish, knowing what awaited me all too soon.

But at least I could do the one thing I'd wanted to do since I'd arrived.

"Iska," I said, "I can't go back, so you have to tell the others for me. Don't go there. It's not worth it. The Light will take everything from you."

"How much is everything?" Iska asked.

I did not have the heart to give him an honest answer.

"Like, your listening," I said. "You'll hear less. I almost forgot how to hear my way here. And the ability to leave. I can't go back. I want to go back, but I can't."

What foolishness kept me from running?

Iska looked solemn. "I'll tell them. But are you sure you can't come back?"

"I'm sure," I said.

"Will I see you again?" Iska asked.

"Probably not," I admitted.

"Then I'll hang out until you have to go back," Iska said.

I was touched. "Thank you, Iska."

I didn't realize until then how much I missed Iska's company, how much I missed a familiar voice.

"I should have asked," Iska said. "Who's your friend?"

"I should have introduced you," I said. "Iska, this is Halmo. He's one of the main engineers who keeps the Light working. Halmo, this is Iska, my best friend since I was learning to walk."

Iska reached out, clapping a hand on Halmo's shoulder. I felt Halmo flinch under my hand. "Hey! Nice to meet you!"

"Um...an honor to meet you," Halmo said.

"They're not very touchy-feely there," I explained to Iska. "I think it's because they can see where you are."

"Oh!" Iska brought his hand away. "Sorry about that."

"No, it's fine," Halmo said. "I only just met Kimi. Otherwise I'm sure I would know all about you."

"We're about the same person anyway," Iska said. "If you know Kimi, you know me."

"That is so not true!" I said.

"Okay, even your mom can't tell us apart sometimes," Iska said.

"My mom just says that," I said. "Otherwise she'd blame you when we run out of chitinbread. But no, she always knows to blame me."

"That's because it usually is you!" Iska said.

"Well, yeah, that's fair," I said.

"What's chitinbread?" Halmo asked.

"It's a hard tack made with ground-up beetles," Iska said. "It's supposed to be a hard-times food, and Kimi's the only person who likes it."

I didn't like it that much, really. I mostly ate it because it amused everyone else. But saying it would have ruined the joke.

But I wished now that I had not mentioned chitinbread. No matter how bad it tasted, it was a familiar flavor, and now I wanted nothing more than a crumb of a flavor I knew.

"How long are you here?" Iska asked.

"Not that long," I said. "Oh. Halmo, I wanted to show you something before we go. Iska, you know that big cavern with the really good echoes?"

"Yeah, of course," Iska replied.

"Halmo's never had to listen for his steps before," I said. "He just goes by sight."

"What, really?" Iska asked.

"Yeah, really," I said. "I thought we could show him the cave, and he could try listening there."

"Okay, sure," Iska said. "I can tag along, right?"

"Yeah, of course," I said. "It's not much farther, Halmo. It's part of this same cave complex."

Halmo trusted me a little more now, enough to let me lead him. He never hesitated, never slowed down. I made sure he never stumbled.

And then we reached it. It was a fairly boring cave, really. It was mostly big, with surfaces that echoed well. It was great for kids who were still developing their ears, but when you got older you realized there was too little variation in the surfaces. Still, even here, the sounds changed more than in the retraining room.

"Look at this!" Halmo breathed.

"So, this is where we bring kids to learn how to listen," I told Halmo. "What you do is…well, you have a lantern, so you have to close your eyes. And then you need to make sound. Stomp, clap, sing, whatever you want. And then you listen for the echo."

Halmo didn't move at first. Then he shifted his grip on the lantern so he could clap.

I heard the clap well enough. It bounced off of every surface. I could hear the near perfect dome shape of this cave.

"Okay, good," I said. "What did you hear?"

"An echo…" Halmo said.

"Yeah, what's the shape of the room?" I said. "Without opening your eyes."

"I don't know."

"Oh wow," Iska said. "He really hasn't listened before."

"No," I said. "None of them have. Um, okay. Halmo, let go of my hand. I'm going to—or, no. Iska. Could you move away and start talking?"

"Sure," Iska said. He ran a couple of paces. "Is that good?"

"Yes," I said. "Halmo, you can hear where he is, right? You need to go toward his voice."

Halmo didn't move.

"This way, mate!" Iska said. "Come on, you can do it!"

Halmo stepped. He was facing far, far to the left of Iska.

"Nope, not there," Iska said. "Where are you going?"

"Can you not hear where he is?" I asked.

"No, I can't," Halmo said. "I can't hear well."

"You're deaf?" I asked.

"Not fully," Halmo said. "Only partly. Mostly in my left ear. I hear...for example, water. In my right ear it sounds almost normal, maybe a little quiet. But in my left ear it sounds like music to me, echoey and metallic with defined notes."

"Metallic?" I repeated.

"Yes," Halmo said. "So, I only hear clearly in one ear, and if ears work like eyes, you need two working ears for depth perception. And in places with too much sound, I cannot hear anything except the background noise."

"Well, still," I said. "That's going to make it hard for you to learn echolocation. Sorry."

"What do you do if someone can't hear?" Halmo asked.

"We take care of them," I said. "But there's other ways to navigate. If you can't hear, you can go by feel. I know one person who can smell her way."

"Yeah, it's wild," Iska said. "She can smell the difference between caves, and she can tell who you are by your smell. It's kinda freaky actually. Like, it makes me wonder—how do I smell to someone like that?"

"Hmm," Halmo said.

The light grew a little dimmer.

"Kimi," Halmo said, "I'm sorry. We need to go back."

"Oh," Iska said, disappointed. "You take care, Kimi, okay? Come back if you can."

"I will if I can," I said.

"Iska," Halmo said. "That's your name, right?"

"Yeah," Iska said.

"Could I meet you again at the glowworm cave in a few days?" he asked. "Around nighttime?"

"What's nighttime?" Iska asked.

"It's when people are asleep," Halmo said.

"They all sleep at the same time," I explained to Iska. "They have this bright light that they dim, and then they all go to sleep at the same time."

"All at once?" Iska asked.

"Yeah," I said.

"And they dim light..." Iska said, not understanding.

"Kinda like how...you know how on the surface it's bright if it's dangerous and dark if it's safe?" I said. "Kinda like that but less so."

"You go to the surface?" Halmo asked, startled.

"Yeah, sometimes," I said. "Not much. It depends how bad the storms are, where we're going up."

"You didn't tell me that!" Halmo said.

"There wasn't a reason to know," I said. "You never go to the surface?"

"No, because it isn't safe!" Halmo said. "Iska, I don't think I can get Kimi out again any time soon, but could you show me how you go to the surface? And why?"

"Yeah, sure," Iska said. "But I'm still not sure when."

"Do you have a timekeeping device?" Halmo asked. "And does it track hours?"

"I think so, yes," Iska said.

"Six hours from now," Halmo said. "I'll be back in six hours."

"I'll check back by the glowworms once in a while," Iska said.

"I'll bring an hourglass for you," Halmo said. "Then we can coordinate using that."

"Iska, show him the glowing mushrooms," I added. "And the glowing rocks. That will give him ideas."

"Glowing rocks?" Halmo repeated.

"Yeah, only if they've seen enough sunlight," I said. "After a while they stop glowing. But they're every color."

The light grew dimmer. Halmo cranked at it until it held a steady light.

"We really have to go back, Kimi," Halmo said.

"Yeah, alright," I said. "Iska—" I hesitated, and I felt as if my feet were rooted to the spot. "Iska, it was really good to see you again."

"You really don't want to go back," Iska said.

"No, I don't," I said.

"Then stay here with us," Iska coaxed.

"I can't," I said.

Iska threw his arms around me. I threw my arms around him.

"We really miss you, Kimi," Iska said. "You know that."

"I miss all of you too," I said.

Iska held me for a full minute before he let me go. Halmo took my hand again.

"Stay safe," Iska said.

"Yeah, you too," I said.

We started back, and silence swallowed us.

"It's not fair to you," Halmo said. "Keeping you from that, I mean."

"Yeah, I miss them," I said.

"No wonder," Halmo said. "But even your culture. We must be so strange to you."

"Yeah, you are," I said. "But we must be pretty strange to you too."

"In a wonderful way," Halmo said.

Even from a distance, the entrance to the Light glowed, even though it was only open a crack. It hurt to look toward the sharp rectangular outline. How colossally different from the glowworms we had been admiring only minutes ago. As we grew closer, I started to hear the whirring but I did not hear it in full until Halmo pulled the door open. It was not muffled by the door's shrill squeak.

I did not want to step in, but step in I did, and I felt my heart grow heavier in my chest.

And then I froze. I could hear where I was, but in that short time I'd somehow forgotten how disorienting such intense light could be.

All of this light from one person?

I heard the door jam sharply into place and jumped. Even without turning, there was something uncomfortable about now being fully trapped so close to the Light.

Halmo took my hand, gently leading me back to the other room.

"How well can you keep a secret, Kimi?" Halmo asked.

"I can keep one," I said.

"We are not going to tell Burgiss anything," Halmo said.

"Why not?" I asked.

"Because," Halmo said, "Burgiss has never been able to keep a secret to save his life. It was secret enough that engineers have ways outside, and he knew he shouldn't be talking about that openly. You're now carrying secrets that could affect people's lives. That exit's location is supposed to be a secret. And if—if—I start working on changing this Light, if Burgiss finds out, he will be too excited. He will tell the world."

I swallowed.

"So, you won't tell him," Halmo said. "Right?"

"Right," I said.

Halmo opened the door to the outside.

"What took you so long?" Burgiss asked.

"We had a long conversation," Halmo said. "We were talking about how the Light works mechanically, but also different types of light. Different wavelengths and what they do, the composure of the electromagnetic grid…"

"So, boring stuff," Burgiss said.

"Boring stuff," Halmo agreed.

"And you're interested in that?" Burgiss asked.

"Yes," I said. "I mean, I wish it wasn't this, but it's nice knowing how it works anyway."

Burgiss nodded. I saw the sadness in the way he tipped his head.

"Did either of you plan for him to come back?" Burgiss asked.

"Not for a while," Halmo said. "He's welcome back any time, and I'll let you know if I can think of something else to show him."

"Are you ready to go back?" Burgiss asked.

"Not really," I said, "but I guess we have to."

"We have to," Burgiss agreed.

"I'll find a reason for you to come back soon," Halmo said. "It's nice having company here."

"You have your coworkers," Burgiss said.

"Other than them," Halmo said. "We barely talk. Especially since..."

"Yeah," Burgiss said. "You take care of yourself, Halmo."

"The same to you," Halmo said. I wasn't sure if I imagined that he said it with a little too much gravity.

It was harder going back this time, with the memory of stepping outside still so fresh. My ears still noticed the buzzing. My eyes still flinched away from the light.

And when the door creaked open, the symmetry of the room reminded me that no matter how hopeful I was, even if Halmo was brave enough to do something, we really were working to save the next person. This place would be my last home.

# 10

It's funny how that type of knowledge changes how you think and what you do. Things that matter fall away.

There was no being sad. And as Pelus had said, there was no being angry. I wasn't going to change my fate. But I couldn't mistake the way I felt for happiness. It was a burdened joy at best, with a constant grim background.

Chores became mindless monotony. The endlessly repeating schedule was nothing but a weary rhythm. There was nothing to look forward to at this point, except maybe a chance to see Halmo again.

Poor Iska, I thought. He had no idea. At least, I hoped he had no idea.

But what surprised me most was the shadow-snatcher.

The next time he came, I waited in line. Before, I had dreaded this. Now, I knew I was supposed to dread it, but my heart was like stone. This was nothing. It was nothing compared to the Light.

It was nothing.

My heart beat no faster. My palms felt no sweat. My shoulders held no tension. My knees did not tremble.

We stepped forward.

"Hey, Spy," Luchia whispered. "You should tell him what a spy you are."

I ignored her.

"He probably won't know what you're saying though," she added, "because you still talk stupid."

We stepped forward.

"I know you can hear me, Spy," Luchia whispered. "Because you hear everything else. You know Marvus is just using you, right? He doesn't like you any more than anyone else does. He just feels sorry for you."

I ignored her.

"He laughs at you when you aren't here," Luchia said.

I didn't believe her one moment.

And who cared if she was right? It wasn't going to matter in a few months.

The door opened. I went in.

The shadow-snatcher looked no friendlier than before. But somehow, he scared me far less. He really was just someone in fancy clothes, no different than anyone else. And what did it matter anyway? What he said changed nothing.

How nervous I had been before. How much my legs had wobbled. Now, I sat without trouble, my eyes averted.

"What shadow do you have today?" the shadow-snatcher asked.

"I spat on the floor because I was angry," I said.

The lie came out simply. I did not stammer. No anxious laugh came unbidden from my lips. Before, I'd been chastised each time for arrogance that was actually fear. How strange to hear a lie come out of my mouth as easily as a truth.

Because who cared if he saw through it? And who cared what he said in response either way?

"Spit stays in your mouth," the shadow-snatcher said. "You will make people sickly that way."

"I know," I said.

"Meet my eyes," the shadow-snatcher said.

I did. Or, I pretended to. I still could not see where his eyes were.

"My eyes, boy," the shadow-snatcher said. "Here."

I saw where his hand moved and stared vaguely in that direction.

"I want you to think about cleanliness," the shadow-snatcher said. "Keep your spit in your mouth. Wash your hands before you handle someone else's food. You carry sickness that might harm someone else. You must remember that."

"Yes," I said.

"You will pay attention to what you do," the shadow-snatcher said.

"Yes," I said.

"You may go."

I stood and left. How strange to get to the end of this without one comment about how arrogant I was. I was almost disappointed.

"What did you tell him?" Braghin whispered as I passed. "Who do you have to apologize to?"

"Your mom," I whispered back.

Braghin's eyes bulged, and he coughed.

"Kimi," Ossik asked, "were you talking?"

"He was," Braghin said.

"You're not supposed to talk!" Ossik said.

I shrugged.

"This will be part of your record, Kimi," Ossik said, "and if your mentor does not bring it up, I will."

"Alright," I said.

Ossik stepped closer to me. "You know what will happen if you fail."

"I know," I said.

"Kimi—" Marvus spoke up.

"No talking," Ossik warned.

Marvus said nothing.

How little fear I had of him now. What could he do? Punch me? I could take a few bruises.

And he wouldn't anyway. It was only Braghin and Jaim who punched.

For lessons, I felt the exact opposite way. As everything else became less important, the lessons became more important and, somehow, easier to learn. Nothing else mattered. Even the lessons didn't matter, really. But making the council have to explain themselves? That mattered.

I was never going to be able to read. I knew that. Not unless the ink was pressed deeply into the paper. But each day, it had to be imprinted a little less for me to catch the different shapes with my fingertips. I'd memorized the shapes of the letters, and I knew them by motions. In my mind, I imagined the sound something would make traveling through the air in the same shapes, and I understood.

I don't know how many weeks or months passed before Burgiss brought me the welcome news.

"Kimi," Burgiss said, "Halmo wanted to show you something else. We're going to go see him today."

And the thought made the light feel a little less harsh for a moment.

As we made our way there, I told myself to temper what I felt. It would be nothing. Something small. Maybe it really would be just one more aspect of how the Light worked. It would be nothing so hopeful as I wanted to think.

How clearly I noticed the buzzing around me again.

Burgiss knocked on the door, and Halmo opened it.

"Kimi," Halmo said, "come in."

I stepped in.

"Did you want to wait?" Halmo asked.

"Yes," Burgiss said firmly.

"We'll be back soon," Halmo said. "This will not take as long as last time."

Halmo closed the door.

"I can't show you in here," Halmo said. "But I can show you outside."

We reached the exit, and Halmo threw his weight against it. It opened far more easily this time, heavily but without complaint.

"I put some oil on it," Halmo said. "If I'm using it often, it has to work properly."

The cool darkness swept around us, and a gentle silence extended its welcome.

But the darkness was not so entire anymore.

Not far away, there was a container. Glass, maybe? Sound bounced off of it like stone. But inside, there was light. It was a very blue light, with hints of orange and green.

My jaw dropped.

"Iska and I have been hard at work on this project," Halmo said.

I crept closer to it. As I grew closer, I heard a faint buzzing. If I held a hand near enough the glass, I felt a faint warmth.

"Is it..." I couldn't find the right word.

"It's a prototype," Halmo said. "Most of the visible light comes from bioluminescent creatures and fungi. Iska showed me most of them. Some I never knew existed."

"It still buzzes," I said.

"It would have to buzz anyway," Halmo said. "People will notice if the sound disappears. But even if that wasn't a concern, it still needs to produce ultraviolet light so we can absorb the right vitamins into our skin, and it needs to produce warmth for some of our greenhouses. Although not as much as people think."

"They don't?" I asked.

"The greenhouses are mostly heated by rabbits," Halmo said. "Rabbits produce so much heat, there's almost no need for the heat generated from the Light. So, I can cut back on that, and if anyone notices, I can add it back in. Either way, with this model, if I could replicate it on a large scale, it would never need a sacrifice again."

I didn't think my jaw could drop further. Perhaps it shouldn't have. It made my jaw-hinge hurt.

"But how is it fueled?" I asked, rubbing my jaw.

"Iska showed me this pond algae," Halmo said. "It replicates itself so fast. It would not be enough to power our Light. But here, if we grow it, so long as we add a steady supply, it will serve as a food source for some of this light biome. And when it dies...actually, that came from a failed prototype earlier. When it dies, it decays, and when it decays, it uses up the oxygen, and the whole biome dies. But if we use the dead algae, if we use up the materials that would decay, that can power the electrical part of the prototype Light. The only problem that leaves is that we would need to constantly be adding more algae, and long-term we might need to breed some of the other lifeforms outside the Light in case one life-form falters for any reason."

"So, it's usable?" I asked.

"Almost," Halmo said. "There are still a few problems with it. The first one, well, you can see it. The light's still very sickly. It's very blue. I can add some red into it with the electricity, but right now, the algae produces only just enough power."

"And the other problem?" I asked.

"It's fragile," Halmo said. "The biome is so finely balanced right now. It was actually better balanced a few hours ago. It needs a few more lifeforms to be fully stable so that if one falters, another can take its place. Or if one overbreeds, another will keep its effects in check."

"I understand," I said.

Halmo nodded.

"So," I said, "does that mean...are you going to try to..."

Halmo took in a breath. "Yeah. Yeah, I'm going to. If I plan it right, no one's going to notice. My coworkers have just about given up. They just look for broken and corroded wires these days and that's it, and the wires will look and work about the same. They can barely see what's going on with so much light in their eyes anyway."

"And how long do you think it will take?" I asked.

"We're still in early stages," Halmo said reluctantly, "so it's hard to tell. I'm going to start...I'm hoping in a week or two I'm going to start the replacement, even though it's not fully ready. Just to test. And I'm going to test in that room you and Burgiss come through. No one goes there anyway. And if it works there, I'm still thinking it's going to be at least a year. In the best case scenario, I'd say a little under a year. Two or three years if it doesn't work well."

I felt a little of my elation die down.

"For the next person," I said.

"Yes," Halmo said. "For the next person." He brought a hand to the glass. "And for everyone else too."

I said nothing.

"I'm not doing this without a selfish intention," Halmo said. "I was there when my mentor slipped when working on a broken section of the Light. It was a small mistake. He simply brushed the wrong wire. And once that happened, it was too late. There was nothing I could do except finish the repair. And I know if the Light isn't changed, the same thing will happen to me someday, one day when I work too hastily or had too little sleep, or when I've been working a little too long that day." He brought his hand away from the glass. "We're doing this for everyone."

"Except the council," I said.

"Even them," Halmo said. "Yes, they derive power from it, and it's shameful. Some of them delight in it. But others, I think they simply don't know how to function without the threat of the Light, and they won't know until they have no choice."

"Hmm," I said.

"There's one more thing I wanted to try, Kimi," Halmo said. "Iska said that there was a place you both found as boys. You went together, but only once. He says he doesn't remember how to get there, but he thought you did."

"I probably don't," I said. "Iska and I went everywhere. We probably gave our parents headaches with how far we used to wander."

"Do you remember a place where the water stretched farther than you could hear," Halmo said, "and the water glowed when you touched it?"

I remembered vividly. I hadn't thought of it in years.

"Yes, I do," I said.

"Do you remember where it is?" Halmo asked.

I thought. "Vaguely," I said. "I went there a few other

times alone. It scared Iska too much. He fell into the water, and he thought all of the light creatures would eat him. I pulled him out, but he was soaked to the skin long after we got back."

"Can you show me?" Halmo asked. "Not today, but another day."

"Sure, I'll try," I said.

"I'll see if we can have a full day," Halmo said. "So, that's another thing I have done since last time. When I went with Iska to the surface, I noticed that our day-night cycle does not match the day-night cycle on the surface. I'm sure it used to match, but over time, maybe our clocks were a little faster, or we changed how many hours we were awake or asleep. Now they no longer match."

"And that means..." I said.

"It means that some of our 'days' match up with the surface's 'night,'" Halmo said. "I calculated it out, and in a few weeks, they match enough, and they will match for some time. But they'll only match for some time before they fall out of sync again."

"How are you going to convince Burgiss?" I asked.

"He won't need any convincing," Halmo said. "He's happy for any excuse to get you out of there for some time. But I have an idea anyway."

Back inside, the buzzing and the Light still felt like a rude interruption from the outside, but they felt a little less intrusive this time. Its power felt less harsh with the new knowledge that it would soon be gone.

Outside, Burgiss waited.

"What did you show him that took so little time?" Burgiss asked.

"It was more to correct something," Halmo said. "I misexplained something before. But I wanted to work with Kimi on something in a few weeks, something to improve his math skills. It will take me some time to gather the materials, so if he's available in a few weeks, I'll be ready."

"How long will you need?" Burgiss asked.

"A whole day if possible," Halmo said, "but at least a half day."

"A whole day?" Burgiss repeated. "I'll see if we can get it."

I stepped out.

"Take care, Burgiss," Halmo said.

"You too," Burgiss replied.

Halmo started to close the door, but Burgiss caught it.

"Halmo," Burgiss said, "I don't know what you are teaching Kimi, but thank you. He seems so much happier."

"I think the math calms him," Halmo said. "He thinks about it differently, as you said, but I think it grounds him."

"I don't fully understand," Burgiss said, "but I think it makes sense."

"You have to teach him the reading and writing part," Halmo said. "I don't know how you are doing that."

"We have a method," Burgiss said. "Right, Kimi?"

"Right," I said.

"He learns so fast," Burgiss said. "He learns fast the way you learn. I just wish the council would see that."

"They will see," Halmo said. "Perhaps too clearly, Burgiss."

"What does that mean?" Burgiss asked.

"I don't pretend to understand the council's intentions," Halmo said, "but...out here I don't want to say more, but I think you know what I mean."

"I don't," Burgiss said.

"Don't be stubborn, Burgiss," Halmo said. "How happy do you think they will be to see your student of all people learning more readily than a council member's son?"

I heard Burgiss's foot shift.

"Ah—" Burgiss started.

"But don't say more out here," Halmo said.

"I see your point," Burgiss said.

"Don't stop teaching him by any means, Burgiss," Halmo said, "but don't expect a miracle either."

"I don't expect one," Burgiss said. But I heard the sorrow in his undertones.

"Kimi, in a few weeks I'll be all set," Halmo said. "See you then."

He closed the door.

Burgiss didn't move.

"Burgiss?" I asked.

"Yes?" he said.

"Are you alright?"

"Yeah," he said. "I'm just thinking through how to ask for a full day. I think I can do it."

## 11

For weeks I waited with baited breath. I struggled through lessons and muddled through everything else. Burgiss was ever-patient, and Marvus kept me company when things were hardest. Days when knowledge weighed too heavily. Nights when I could not find the will to stand up for myself.

And then one day, Burgiss came with the news.

"Okay, they finally agreed," Burgiss said. "I talked to Halmo again, and next week you'll go see him. Okay?"

"Okay," I said. "Thanks, Burgiss."

Waiting through that week was painful, but finally, we made our way back. Maybe I was imagining things, but when the door opened, the light past it seemed a little less harsh than usual.

"Ready?" Halmo asked me.

"Yes," I said.

"Then come on in," Halmo said.

I went in. Halmo closed the door. The buzzing felt just a little less intense in my ears.

"What do you think?" Halmo asked.

I blinked, confused, then realized. "This is the prototype Light?"

"Yes, it is," Halmo said. "It's more stable now. Still finicky, but better than I expected."

"It doesn't hurt as much," I said.

"I'm not surprised the Light hurts," Halmo said. "I wonder if you see it differently. I notice some of the difference, but only barely. If Burgiss noticed, he didn't say."

"Maybe he'll say something when we get back," I said.

"If he doesn't," Halmo said, "then if that prototype stays stable, it works. I still want to see your glowing creatures, though, in case they are more stable. Some of the creatures in there are mostly useful in a larval form, and if I can swap them out for something else, that would make the prototype more viable."

Halmo grabbed his lantern, winding it, and then we made our way through the exit. It scarcely resisted opening this time.

"I'll use the lantern as a timer," Halmo said. "After three turns, even if we haven't reached it, we have to go back."

"It's far," I said, "but I don't think it's that far."

"Then we'll have time to talk on the way," Halmo said. "Unless that distracts you."

"No," I said. "More noise means I can hear better where we are going."

"If we talk about math," Halmo said, "then if you bring that back, it might be one more way to show the council how foolish they are."

"Yeah, sure," I said.

"I did not expect that response," Halmo said. "Usually one mention of math sends people groaning."

"Really?" I asked.

"Usually," Halmo said. "Haven't you seen Burgiss's response?"

I laughed. "Yeah, he really doesn't like math."

So, we talked. We bounced ideas off of each other. Some were new to me. Some were new to him. More often than not, we knew the same concept in different ways. We counted differently. I counted to twelve on my finger joints; Halmo counted to ten on his fingers. I thought in fractions; he thought in decimal points. I thought of distance in time and sound, like the return of an echo; he thought of it in increments and sight, like placing a finger on either side of a rock. And once, we paused our chatter so Halmo could wind his lantern again.

At one point I stopped, listening. I found the rock I was looking for, and I rubbed my fingers over it. I felt distinct scratches and indents.

"What is that?" Halmo asked.

"It's a marker," I said. "So, this, if you feel it, this is how we write."

He went to it, staring. Then he rubbed his fingers over it.

"Interesting!" he said.

I will not bore you with the rest of our conversations. Mostly we talked about how the Light prototype would work. But we also talked about everything from favorite foods to childhood memories. Before long, I knew Halmo almost as well as I knew Burgiss.

The lamp flickered.

"Two times," Halmo mumbled, turning the crank. "Are we close?"

"I think so," I said. The uncertainty reached my voice, though. Surely it wasn't this far away.

But not much later, I recognized a scent in the air, a briny smell that I'd only found here.

"I think we're almost there," I said. "I recognize this place. That overhang there. Watch your head."

He ducked under.

I found a mark, and I touched it. It was distinct still, less worn than some of our other marks, but crude. It had been made by a child's hand. My hand, five years ago.

"Okay, we have to be a bit careful," I said. "Sometimes the large water is higher and sometimes lower."

I could hear it now, rushing back and forth.

"Okay, it's lower right now," I said.

The cavern dropped sharply here, and I moved carefully. This was how Iska had fallen in before. He'd lost his footing, and the water was high.

We emerged by a drop of a few feet. We were in the ceiling of a round-roofed cave, far wider than it was tall. As a child, I'd been able to stand up. At my size now, I would have to crouch.

I dropped down. Halmo dropped next to me. He was reduced to a crawl.

"This had better be worth it," Halmo muttered.

As we made our way to the front of the cave, it opened a little more. Before us spread a narrow bar of rocky shore. And then, beyond, the enormous water, spread under a dark sky.

We'd come at just the right time of year. The water was glowing bright blue.

"Wow," Halmo breathed.

"Cool, isn't it?" I said.

"Wow," Halmo said again.

"And that isn't all," I said.

"What is the creature or plant that glows so brightly?" he asked.

"I don't know," I said. "I can't see it well. I think it might just be the water."

"I heard a story once," he said. "On the surface, there was a place with water so big that you could not see the edge of it. It was supposed to be filled with salt and gold and other precious things. And it was supposed to be filled with life, so much life, and such varied life that not even the most vivid imagination could do this place justice. It held enough food to feed a thousand nations, and it held beings as large as gods that survived by eating creatures so tiny that you almost could not see them with the naked eye. And these tiny creatures—krella I think they were called—they were supposed to be so numerous and reproduce so quickly that they could feed an ecosystem." He looked over the ocean. "If these are those krella, if they reproduce so rapidly they can feed a place so vast as this, and if they've survived so long even as life seemed to end everywhere else, this could be the answer." He pulled off his backpack. "I need to get a sample."

"They're not all," I said. "There are creatures here even when the krella aren't here. They glow too, but only if you touch them."

"Do they?" he asked.

"Yeah," I said.

I moved to an area where the water was most still, sheltered by a rocky mass that jutted into the expanse. I touched the water, and where I touched, the water flashed. As I moved my hand, more flashes glinted around my hand.

Halmo came to me. He also stuck his hand in the water, watching in amazement as the water lit around him. The water faintly splashed as he drew his hand closer to shore.

An enormously bright flash emanated from the water.

Halmo gasped, pulling his hand away.

"What was that?" I asked.

"I don't know," Halmo said, "but it was slimy."

He reached over, grabbing his lamp. He touched the water again until he found the thing that had flashed.

He laughed. "Look at it! It looks so weird!"

I couldn't see it well enough. Seeing the water was challenge enough.

He reached into his bag and pulled out several containers. He scooped each one into different places in the water. Gingerly, he placed each one back into his pack as if each one held the heart of the world. When they were all tucked away, he didn't move.

"Burgiss would love to see this," Halmo said. "Maybe, maybe when this is all done, maybe I'll bring him here."

It was nice to imagine him here, I thought. How I wished I could show him even the glowworms.

"He'll know eventually, right?" I said. "He'll know when the Light turns into something like this."

"They all will, eventually," Halmo said.

"When it's too late to change it back," I said.

"That's the plan," Halmo said.

We were quiet a while.

"How did you become friends with Burgiss?" I asked.

"That's a good question," Halmo said. "I'm not sure if Burgiss would want me to answer."

"I can ask him," I said.

"He won't answer," Halmo said. "It's the one secret he can keep. It does no harm to tell you, so long as you can keep it secret."

"I can," I said.

"We were classmates," Halmo said. "We didn't get along well. He was a trouble kid, and I was a star student. Both of our paths were set before we were able to have a choice. The day I found out I had an apprenticeship as a Light mechanic, that's the day I found out he was going into retraining. I knew what that meant, but I didn't think much of it at the time. I believed what they said about only the impossibly shadowed people being used to sustain the Light. I believed it until maybe a week after that year's ceremony. It was infamous, Kimi. Everyone was talking about it, about the two shadowed boys who were so evenly matched yet were trying so hard to save each other. If that doesn't start to make you rethink, nothing will.

"A week later, it was my turn to do night maintenance, mostly to make sure everything was still working properly. I heard this strange sound, this thumping sound. So I went to see what it was. It was Burgiss. He was trying to break into the machine."

I blinked. "To save his friend?"

"No," Halmo said. "To throw himself in."

My eyes widened.

"I stopped him," Halmo said. "He wasn't close anyway. It's well-locked. I tried to comfort him, but he was beyond comfort at the time. And he told me about the friend he'd lost...and my view changed." He shrugged. "I couldn't leave my job maintaining the Light's mechanisms. I never really wanted that apprenticeship in the first place, but it was too prestigious for me to pass it up. And now, I can't afford to leave it. I've seen others try to convince people why they'd leave such an important job, or that they have other skills they can use. Even just a few weeks without work would leave me without a place to live or food to eat. It takes a great amount of heart to throw everything away like that." He smiled sadly. "A heart like Burgiss's, really. That's how he's gotten into so much trouble."

"Hmm," I replied.

"You can see why he would not want someone else to know."

"Yeah, no wonder," I said.

We stared a little longer. It was nice to imagine we could just stay here forever, watching the glowing water.

"If the krella works...." Halmo said.

I turned to him.

"No," Halmo said.

"What?" I asked.

"If it works," Halmo said, "it still won't be on time. I don't even know how fast krella reproduce yet, if they'll reproduce. And even if the stories aren't exaggerated..."

"So, on time for the next person," I said.

"The next person," Halmo mumbled. "But...I know it's unrealistic. I want to find some way that it will be done on time for you."

"How much time is left?" I asked.

"Not enough," Halmo said.

"Not enough," I agreed.

We fell silent.

The lamp flickered.

"Time to go back," Halmo said, picking up the pack. "Can you help me get it back up there?"

"Sure," I said. "There's a bit of a slope here for a foothold."

"You climb up first," Halmo said, "and I'll pass it up to you."

Climbing back up had been a little harder as a kid. But now, my arm strength plus the foothold was enough to get me back up on the ledge. It helped that the ledge was at shoulder height now. Halmo passed me the bag, then struggled up, catching his head and his shoulder on the low overhang.

"I can carry it if you want," I offered.

He pulled it onto his back. "I have it."

How quiet we were going back, at least at first.

"I really hope Burgiss sees that place someday," I said eventually.

"Yeah, me too," Halmo said.

"What do you think he'll say?" I asked.

"I don't know," Halmo said. "I don't think he'll want to talk."

"Why not?" I asked.

"Because," he said, "I can't bring him there without telling him that you showed it to me."

"Yeah," I said.

"Can you think of any other places you've seen?" Halmo asked. "Places that you might remember but Iska might not?"

"Not really," I said. "Most of them are places everyone else knows. That's the only one I can think of. And I'm not the only person who knows about it. It's just most people don't want to walk this far."

"No wonder," Halmo replied. "My feet are tired." He shifted the pack. "And this does not help."

The lantern flickered.

"Two more hours," Halmo said.

"Do you want me to carry it?" I asked.

"No, I've got it," Halmo said.

"Well, the offer is there," I said.

"You're carrying enough," Halmo said.

I spread my hands. "I'm carrying nothing."

"Nothing except for everything," Halmo said.

I had no response.

We made it back in one hour and a half. I knew as soon as we saw the little prototype light outside. It still glowed, although it was fainter now.

Halmo pulled his pack off, gingerly lowering it to the ground. He pulled out one of the jars. It still glowed.

"I'll have to analyze some of the water," he said. "If this works, I'll need to replicate the environmental conditions so the krella survive, and I might need more samples of the water for that. I think I remember how to get back there. Are you sure no one else knows how to get there?"

"I'm sure Iska could remember if pressed," I said. "He's afraid of it, but I think he remembers more than he thinks."

"I hope he does," Halmo said. "If so, the two of us together can figure it out." He rubbed at his back.

"I could have carried it partway," I said.

"And as I said," Halmo said, "you are carrying enough."

He opened the door back in. In the waiting room, the light was noticeably dimmer and a little greener with noticeable orange.

"And this is what I mean about this not being stable," he said. "Which is why if the krella…"

He grabbed some tools, and he pulled open a panel.

"Let's see," he said. "For temporary, I'll just adjust this. That will increase some of the blue light for now. Do I have more…let me check."

He left, then came back holding a container of something glowing. I heard him open something else.

"Okay, I'm not sure if you see what I'm doing, Kimi," Halmo said. "Burgiss says your eyesight's poor."

"I can't see what you did," I said. "I just hear you moving things."

"I'm adding some more glowworms," he said. "Just in this area. It's not really enough, but it will take some of the strain off of the electronic light. Back there, I'm not sure if you can see. I found a few mushrooms that glow in the red range. They don't do much, though. Most of the red range light is electronic. But the creatures in here cover most of the other ranges, from yellow down to blue." I heard something click. "Okay, how does that look to you?"

"Less green," I said.

"Let me see." Halmo stood. "Yes, much better."

He closed the panel.

"But if I can't keep the color and intensity right for more than a few hours," Halmo said, "it's enough to work in place of the Light but not enough to keep us from being caught before it's in place." He sighed. "I just wish it would come together faster!"

"Well, hey," I said. "Where did we start? We didn't start with anything. And now, look at this. You have a whole room that doesn't need the Light. That has to count for something. Right?"

"It's farther than I thought we'd be three months ago," Halmo said.

"It's been three months?" I asked.

"Something like that," Halmo said. "Yes."

That thought landed heavily.

"If the krella work as well as I think they will," Halmo said, "then we'll be even farther." He stepped closer to the prototype, and I heard his fingers brush over the glass. "And the day I can link all of this into the Light's systems and start pulling out its most dangerous pieces, that is going to be a beautiful day."

It was going to happen, I told myself. Someday.

# 12

Time was moving too fast now, and the faster it moved, the worse my nightmares became.

One sticks out vividly in my mind.

In my dream, two people led me to a strange room. The sound bounced off the walls in a bizarre, warped way. The walls bent in alien curves, not at all like a cavern. Not even like stalactites. They bent in eldritch, organic shapes, and the sound bounced almost soft. The walls were moving. They were breathing.

And the people were watching, eerily still. They were breathing with the walls.

And then they were singing. And so was the cavern. It was a haunting, beautiful melody, the type of song you do not remember at first but somehow remember more and more over time. Your heart remembers even when your mind does not. And the two people and I walked silently, our steps matching the slow rhythm of the music.

The two people opened a door, and they pushed me through.

The world was white. Cold metal pressed into me but especially into my arm. The whiteness grew brighter. I felt as if every piece of me was slowly fading away, and the whiteness became all-consuming. I was the whiteness, and I felt how I touched everything around me. All of me except my arm, where the pressure was firmer. It was warm.

"Kimi," Marvus's voice whispered, "wake up."

My eyes opened. I was in bed. The Light was as dulled as it ever became. Marvus's hand was on my arm.

"Are you alright?" Marvus asked.

"Yeah," I said. "Why?"

"You were yelling in your sleep," Marvus said.

"I was?" I asked.

"Yeah," Marvus said.

"Yeah, you were yelling for your mommy," Braghin said.

"No, you weren't," Marvus said. "I don't know what you were saying."

"You were yelling like a little baby," Braghin said. "Are you going to cry, little baby?"

"Don't listen to him," Marvus said. "It sounded like you had a really scary dream."

"Yeah," I said.

"What was it?" Marvus asked. "Do you want to talk about it?"

"No," I said.

"Alright," Marvus said.

He climbed back down.

"I hope your dream comes back, little baby," Braghin said.

"Oh, shut up," Marvus said.

"It's fine, Marvus," I said.

I pulled my pillow over my head to block out anything else they said.

—

The morning after that dream, I met with Halmo. Before Burgiss he was composed, but the moment the door closed, he smiled broadly.

"Do you want to see the newest prototype?" he asked.

"Yeah, I do!" I replied.

As I followed him, I could hear the excitement in his footsteps. He walked so fast I almost stumbled keeping up.

And when I saw it, I knew this was the final one. How bold the light appeared. How bright, only subtly less bright than the Light. The buzzing was just that little bit quieter.

"What do you think?" Halmo asked.

"It's incredible!" I said.

"I made it a few weeks ago," Halmo said, "and it's been stable all of this time. The light quality has stayed the same. The biome only needs a little care once in a while. Is there anything else you think we need to track?"

"I mean, there's the sound," I said. "It's a little quieter, but not much."

"They won't notice the difference if I implement it right," Halmo said. "You said the sound is about the same, right?"

"Yeah, it's really close," I said. "It's only a little quieter, but it's the same pitch."

"And the light quality is similar," Halmo said. "And the combination of the algae and the krella, they both reproduce so rapidly, and their lifespans are so short, their remains are more than enough to power it. They're so carbon-rich. And Kimi, here's the exciting part. I've started adding it into the main system."

"You have?" I asked.

"Yes," Halmo said. "I started earlier this week. Here and there, where people will notice least."

"And how long will it take from here?" I asked.

Halmo sighed, and his shoulders sagged. "It kills me, Kimi. We're months ahead of schedule thanks to the krella. We're so close, but I'm still...I still think it's going to be one or two months too late. In the best case, still, I'd be two weeks too late. Two weeks! If we'd just caught the krella a month or two earlier, we'd be on time."

"Still," I said, "we've got it. It's close. And it'll be done in a month or two, right? The idea was to be on time for the next person."

"It was," Halmo said. "And it will be. And by then, I'll have figured out how to disable the pieces of the Light that..."

". . . yeah," I finished. I hesitated. "It's...how long does it take? It feeds a whole year?"

"Kimi," Halmo said, "why do you want to talk about that now?"

"Well, it's coming up, isn't it?" I said. "I want to be prepared. How long does it take?"

"It's...oh, for you?" Halmo said. "It's instant. Living Light! What did you think it was going to be?"

"I didn't know," I said. "I only knew that it feeds on living cells for a year."

"Living Light, no!" I heard Halmo take in a breath. "No, it does not leave you conscious. It uses your cells and their capacity to divide and redivide, but it doesn't need your consciousness to do that. We're desperate, Kimi, but we're not cruel." Halmo hesitated. "Or perhaps we are."

I wanted to cheer Halmo up. But how did I answer that honestly?

"I'll work as fast as I can, Kimi," Halmo said, "but don't expect any miracles. I don't think I can replace enough of the Light fast enough to be able to shut down the worst part of it on time."

"I know," I said.

"My plan is to leave as much of the Light still functioning as possible," Halmo said. "The yearly date is not a hard-and-fast rule. It's just to make sure the Light does not run out of energy. It will keep working for a short time after even without fuel. It's just a matter of calculating how much I can replace before it runs out. All it takes is a few minutes of darkness in a single room and they'll investigate."

"I know," I said.

I stared at this prototype as long as I could before finally we had to go back.

"The prototype will replace the Light, Kimi," Halmo said before he opened the door. "You can at least be certain of that."

"I know," I said again.

"And when the time comes," Halmo said, "I will make sure that everyone knows that you built this. That you found the krella. That you did a good third of the calculations."

I knew Halmo intended that to give me comfort, even though it provided none.

"Thank you," I said, ignoring the unsettled feeling in my stomach.

—

One morning, after a less memorable version of those nightmares, I woke up groggy. I distantly noticed that my eyes hurt less than usual. At long last, they were getting used to all of this constant brightness.

Still, I had to be out of the room before Braghin and Jaim woke, so I still climbed out of bed quickly. I was ready to go before I knew it.

I glanced back at Marvus and was surprised that he had barely sat up.

"Marvus," I urged. "Come on, let's go."

"Um...yeah," Marvus said.

I waited until he was ready. We were so slow that the other two boys were awake before we left. And once we left, he was quiet.

I didn't think anything of it. Marvus was usually quiet in the morning. As the adults came in, they too were quiet. I only thought it a relief that neither Ossik nor Dorin were bothering me.

I made my way to the kitchen. It was my turn to make the morning meal. I started gathering things together, moving more slowly than was expected of me. I was putting off using the stove, which still scared me. I was never sure how far to turn the dials. My skin still bore a memory of a burn I'd received early on.

As I worked, it occurred to me that my head hurt a little less than usual. Everything felt a little easier. I almost felt as if I could hear better.

The door to the kitchen opened, and I felt something in my chest relax. I recognized Burgiss's footsteps.

"Good morning, Burgiss," I said.

"Good morning," Burgiss said, a strange quality in his voice.

"What's up?" I asked.

"Nothing," Burgiss said.

"No, something's bugging you," I said.

"It's...let's get the morning meal done first. How much have you done?"

I motioned to what I'd gathered.

"Alright. So, let's finish up."

As we cooked, I noticed that the background buzzing was different. It was lower in pitch, and a little quieter. Was that something to do with the electronics?

And now I realized why my eyes hurt less. The Light was not so bright.

I felt a little hope swell in my chest. Was that Halmo slowly replacing the Light?

But when we served the meal, I knew something else was wrong. Everyone was quiet. I felt an urge to break the silence, but I didn't dare. The quiet felt so much gentler on my ears than the constant sound, and the release from the boys' berations was too good to be true.

I did not dare speak until we were in the back room.

"So," I finally said once the door closed, "what's going on?"

"Did you notice the Light?" Burgiss asked, his voice hushed.

"Yeah," I said. "Kinda."

"It's dimmed," Burgiss said.

"I noticed that," I admitted.

Pelus opened the door.

"The Light is usually dimmer this time of year," Burgiss said, "but it seems earlier than usual."

"It's not earlier," Pelus said as he closed the door. "It only feels earlier to you. It's about on schedule."

Any hope I had died, and instead something turned in

my stomach.

"Does it mean anything?" I asked.

"It means that the Light is starting to run out of energy," Pelus said. "Some years it's earlier. Some it's later. Rarely, we have a year where it does not seem to dim at all."

"I thought it wouldn't this year," Burgiss said.

"Either way," Pelus said, "it wouldn't change what time of year this is."

Burgiss's hand came to my shoulder. I knew he intended it to be comforting, but instead I felt the knot in my stomach tighten.

"They've got to see how much Kimi's learned," Marvus said.

"How badly do you wish it, Marvus?" Pelus asked.

"Badly," Marvus said.

"At what cost?"

Marvus was silent.

The tightness of my stomach turned into a rush of terror. I found myself staring silently at the ground. The light seemed brighter, and the room was too small.

I needed air.

Before I could get to my feet, Burgiss's arms came around me. I wanted to push away. Didn't he understand that I needed air?

But instead, my body seemed to go limp. I was shaking.

"Kimi," Burgiss said, "think of five things you can touch."

I blinked, bewildered.

"It will help," Burgiss said.

I tried to think. The cave floor. Burgiss's shirt. My own shirt.

Some of the pain had left my head. I thought I was shaking a little less.

"Then think of four things you can...or, no, you can't see. Four things you can hear."

Burgiss's voice. My voice. That ever-present buzzing.

I felt a heavy shudder run through me.

"Let him wait it out," Pelus said.

Burgiss said nothing, waiting. Pelus and Marvus were quiet. Slowly, I felt the shaking ease away. My legs no longer wanted to run, and my lungs were able to hold enough air.

And now a pain was starting in my head, blunt and deep.

I pulled away from Burgiss. He let go. I brought a hand to my head.

"Are you alright?" he asked.

I laughed, rubbing at the side of my head.

"What I mean is," Burgiss said, "I don't know if you've had a panic attack before."

"Um...no," I said.

"Then I envy you for having gone so long without one," Burgiss said. "But if you have one again, if you feel it's about to happen, there are two ways to fight it. If you're fast enough, you can stave it off by focusing on your senses."

"Yeah, that really didn't work," I said.

"Then sometimes," Burgiss said, "what works for me is taking that fear and turning it into anger. Stare your fear in the eyes and remind it that you're in charge of your mind. If you take offense at your own fear, it's tiring, but it's easier to be tired and angry than to be tired and frightened."

"Burgiss," Pelus cautioned, "you know where your anger gets you."

"I know," Burgiss said, "but in this case, it works."

Pelus moved as if he would say something, but he never said it.

"Halmo said he wanted to review some math with you," Burgiss said. "Look forward to that if nothing else."

"Yeah," I said.

So close, I thought. How close we were to having the Light replaced. How tired I was of keeping it secret. How frustrating to realize we could have been on time.

# 13

Today was the day.

Well, not the day. Tomorrow was the ceremony. But today decided it.

I thought I would be frightened as the day approached. I wasn't. I was calm now, strangely calm. Electrically calm.

Perhaps that was a bad way to put it.

But I was ready, somehow. When the time came, I would be ready.

The last few weeks, I mused, had been easier in some ways. Harder, yes, because the dread carried such a weight that I felt as if I moved through mud. But it was easier too. Everyone else carried a little of the dread too. Dread and hope. Because until the very last day, nothing was guaranteed.

The effect of the dread slowed everyone, I noticed. Even Jaim seemed more distracted. And without Jaim, Braghin's comments whistled with empty air, a little weaker each time. Lessons became fewer. Now, I learned nothing new. I only went over what I already knew.

Because of that, I had been able to do small things in the background. I had to anyway. My nerves would not let me rest. I'd stolen some tinfoil from the kitchen, and I'd been folding it, playing with it, fighting to ignore that rustling sound that made the back of my neck tingle so much. The shadow-snatcher would never have to know. And if he did, it didn't matter.

That morning, it was quieter than usual. Everyone stayed near their mentors and near their friends. Braghin and Jaim were together near the center of the room. Luchia and Aika were a short distance away. Marvus and I were in a corner together.

The wait seemed long and silent. At best, people whispered. Burgiss held my hand. It felt clammy.

The door opened, and the three officials came in.

I didn't recognize them. I had not heard their footsteps in a year. I remembered only now that they wore these long dress-like clothes, not unlike the shadow-snatcher's robes.

"You have reached the end of a very long year," one of them said. "I know you have all been working very hard. Your mentors have given us very high praise of all of you. Better, I would say, than in any previous year."

Why did the sound of his voice trouble me?

"Your mentors all want to see you succeed," the official continued, "and that is why we must evaluate you. Each of you needs to prove what you have learned in this year so we can know if you were successfully retrained."

I felt my hand tighten in Burgiss's hand. He squeezed it.

"We will evaluate you one at a time," the official said, "starting with Braghin."

Braghin stood. They strode as a unit to the back room that we had used for nothing except the shadow-snatcher. The door clicked closed.

And we waited in icy silence.

Before long, the door opened. Braghin came out. He all but sauntered.

I felt a little of the panic starting to rise in me.

Five things you can feel, I told myself. Four things you can hear.

I could feel it subsiding under control.

"Jaim," the official called.

Jaim stood. He went in.

How painful that wait was! I wasn't sure what would be worse, the waiting, the evaluation, or the moment they chose who failed.

How I could feel my heart pulsing, even without the panic.

"You have this, Kimi," Burgiss whispered to me. "You know what you're doing. You've learned everything you could possibly have learned. You've done everything you can."

"Hmm," I mumbled.

Jaim came out. I heard the shakiness of his footsteps.

"Kimi," the official called.

I flinched to hear my name. Burgiss squeezed my hand once more. I stood, and I released my grip from Burgiss's hand. Trembling, I stepped. The distance to that door felt fathoms longer than ever before.

Five things you can feel. Four things you can hear.

I passed the door, and the door closed.

Five things you can feel.

That wasn't working.

Stare it in the eyes.

So, I did. I imagined that deep fear and imagined staring it down. I was in charge, I reminded that fear. And I was not going to make my decisions from a place of fear.

"Please sit, Kimi," one of the officials said as he took his own seat.

I squinted and listened to evaluate. The officials were sitting where the shadow-snatcher had sat before. Before them, to the side, was a chest.

"On this chest, right? I cannot see very well."

"Behind the desk."

I heard the disapproving tone.

"Oh," I said. "I'm sorry. I thought desks were taller."

"This is a sitting desk," the official said.

"Okay," I said. "I'm sorry."

I sat behind it.

"What did you learn this year, Kimi?" the official asked.

My heart pounded so much that I didn't know if my words would form. But then I remembered the shadow-snatcher and how when I understood what was coming, it no longer mattered.

My goal was not to argue for my survival. That would fail. My goal was to make them look bad.

I couldn't think through fear. But I could think through anger.

"They record these evaluations, you know," Burgiss had told me earlier. "They have to so they can compare evaluations later when the decision is difficult. I only know it because so many people have requested to see mine, and they had it."

Maybe they wouldn't keep mine. Maybe they would discard it. And if it didn't matter, why was I afraid?

I felt my fear meet my anger, and somehow, they tempered each other just enough that my mouth opened.

"I learned how to live with the Light," I said. "I came from a place where we lived without light. We lived by our hearing. And because of that, I understood the world differently. Sometimes, my understanding remains flawed, like when I misunderstood that this was a sitting-desk. Before I came here, I did not know what a desk was because we don't use them."

I heard them scratching something.

"When I first came here," I said, "I did not know what a door was. We didn't have doors. You need doors much less when you cannot see. I could barely speak the same language because you have words for things that are foreign to me, and I had words that were foreign to you."

"And how is your understanding different?" the woman official asked.

"Everything is different," I said. "I wear shoes now. I always navigated barefoot, but now I can navigate with shoes. I can think of math in a different way. I can count to ten on my fingers instead of twelve on my finger joints. I can calculate things with decimals instead of fractions.

"And I understand now why the darkness is your enemy. I understand why you need the Light and why you want us to drive out shadows. I did not realize that Light provided so much more than your sight. I didn't realize your food depended on it, and your clean water. No wonder you were so frightened when someone from the darkness came in."

"You say you learned math," the first official said. "We

have a few math problems written in front of you. Can you solve them?"

I felt on the desk in front of me. I felt the paper. I found the pen.

I felt for the numbers. I could feel them ever so faintly, but not enough to trace their shapes.

"I can't feel them enough to read them," I said, "but if they were a little deeper into the paper, or if you spoke them to me, I could solve them."

"Can you recite your times tables?" the second man asked.

"Yes," I said. And I did, only stopping for breath.

I heard silence.

"What is the most complicated math you can do?" the second man asked.

"Trigonometry," I said. "I can draw it if you want."

"How can you draw if you can't see?" the woman asked.

"I can draw and write by feel," I said.

"Show us," the man said.

I took the paper and turned it over.

"So, here," I said. I drew two lines and then one angular line. "So let's say you know this angle." I drew a box around it. "But you want to know this one." I circled another one. "Let me feel...okay, yes, I circled the right one. So this one. If you know this one, and you know that both of these lines are parallel, you can calculate this one too. Both of them have to add up to...it's one eighty here, right? Yeah, okay, that one's the same as for us. And same with these two. And whatever this angle down here equals, so does this one up here." I marked it. "And so..."

"You do not need to say more, Kimi," the second man said. "We're convinced you know math."

"Alright," I said.

"You can also write?"

"Yes," I said. "I can't read because I can't see, but I know by feel how the letters are shaped."

Slowly, carefully, and double-checking with my other hand, I wrote "My name is Kimi."

"That is how I write," I said.

"You must put up with a large amount of ink on your non-dominant hand," the first man said.

"Well, yes," I said.

"And does that ever get into the food you serve your cohorts?" the man asked.

"No," I assured. "I wash my hands very well before I work with food."

One of them came to me and picked up the paper.

"It's a very shaky hand," the woman said. "He writes like a very small child."

"He writes even though he cannot see," the second man said.

"This could make him more dangerous," the woman said. "He comes from shadows, and nothing can change that. Now, he knows enough to exploit the vulnerabilities of the Light."

I swallowed back a curse.

"I understand why you treasure the Light so much now," I said. "But I promise, out there, they wouldn't want anything to do with it. We only were coming here because we were so curious about what light was, but none of us wanted to take it from you. We only came to you the way you might come if you heard an unusual sound and wanted to know what it was. Like if you heard music."

"I see," the second man said.

"You have learned many things, Kimi," the first man said. I heard a tremor of uncertainty in his voice. "We can all acknowledge that. We will take that into our evaluation. But keep in mind, Kimi: it's not about how much you know. It's whether you have accepted the Light into your heart."

Anger overtook fear, and I pulled it back.

"I don't know how to prove that to you," I said. "I have learned how to live as someone lives in the Light. I have learned to understand why you need the Light and why you love the Light so much. I've learned that light can be beautiful. I do not know if there is more you want me to know."

"If you have told us all you can," the second man said, "we will consider what you have told us. You have given us much to think over. You may step out."

I stood. My knees wobbled so much that I fell back down. But then I steeled myself, stood, and staggered my way to the door. I closed the door as quietly as I could, but in the silence, the tiny click held an echo. I felt every person's gaze on me as I sank down next to Burgiss. I felt Burgiss's hand come to my back.

"That took a really long time," Marvus whispered.

"Yeah, it felt like it," I said.

"Their evaluations usually only take a few minutes," Burgiss said, "like Braghin's and Jaim's." He paused. "And they usually call the next person right afterward."

Another minute or two passed before the door opened. "Marvus."

Marvus gulped.

"Go get 'em," I whispered.

I could just see Marvus's weak smile before he turned. And then I only saw his shoulder until he was too far away for me to see clearly.

We waited. The wait felt no shorter, no less heavy. Except that when the door opened again, it did feel too short.

"Luchia," the person called.

Luchia stood. I heard no qualms in her steps.

Marvus sat down with a cross between a groan and a sigh.

"You did it," I said.

"Yeah," Marvus said.

Was now a good time? I wondered. Or did I wait?

"Aika," the person called.

I didn't know, I thought, how long I'd have after Aika's evaluation. Better to do it now.

I reached into my pocket and pulled out the tinfoil symbol I'd been making. It was an eight-pointed star with a gap in the middle, but lines extended inward from each point to a circle. It was lopsided and disproportional, but I knew Marvus would know what it was.

"Hey, Marvus," I whispered, holding it out to him. "I made this for you."

He hesitated before he took it. I felt the star tremble before it came free of my fingers.

"It's not as good as the one your sister made," I whispered, "but it'll do the same thing, right?"

"Kimi..." Marvus said.

"Just do me a favor," I whispered. "Curse the Light once for me, will you?"

Marvus threw his arms around me.

"Oh," I said, bringing my arms around him. "Hey."

I heard his breath. He was crying.

"Easy, Marvus," I said, awkwardly patting his broad back. "It's going to be okay."

He broke away, wiping his eye with the back of his hand.

"How can you say that?" he asked.

He was right. How could I say that?

I shrugged. "I don't know. Maybe it hasn't sunk in yet. But it will be okay. Eventually."

No, it had sunk in. I knew what was coming. And I was ready now. All along, this was what I had been preparing to do.

The door opened, and Aika came out.

And then silence, except for whispering here and there.

"And now?" I asked Burgiss.

"Now," Burgiss said, "we wait for them to decide."

"Alright," I said.

"Kimi," Burgiss said, "whatever happens..." He hesitated. "I know how hollow my words sound. But whatever happens, you have done well, and you've done as well as you could. You're a better student than I am a teacher."

"I wouldn't have learned so much without a good teacher," I said.

Burgiss smiled sadly. "Kimi, I'm a screw-up. I always have been, and I always will be. But you have the potential to be so much more. I only wish they would realize."

I didn't have the heart to tell him that they did realize, and that was the problem.

The door opened. I heard everyone stand. I stood too.

"We will give our decision in the ceremony room," one official said.

The officials left first. Burgiss took his hand firmly in mine. Although we all were slow to leave, Marvus, Pelus, Burgiss and I were last.

How long this walk seemed to be. How weighty each step felt. Had I really been brought this far before, that first day I arrived?

How this place echoed. How intensely I noticed those echoes, so intense that the loudness of the sound fell on my ears with the texture of sandpaper. And entwined around it, that ever-present buzzing.

And maybe the light was dimmer now, but it felt brighter than ever.

My heart picked up speed as we reached the doorway.

Stare it in the eyes.

So, I did. I imagined myself staring it down. That stare pulsed in my head.

We stepped into that room I had not heard in a long, long time. Bright white. We stopped before a platform. The three officials already stood on it. Two men stood before the platform.

"The decision this year was a difficult one," the first official said. "We had many thoughts to consider, and the

Light seems to have reached this year's class a little more than in some previous years. Most of you have grown beyond what we expected. But in the end, it was clear which one person among you was least able to let the Light in."

I did not believe it one moment. They probably said this every year.

"These are unusual circumstances," he said, "but all of you have learned well. Some of you better than your mentors."

Burgiss flinched.

"Knowing this," he said, "we made a decision that tradition would not normally allow."

Two men came toward us, and my chest realized before my mind what was about to happen.

They each took one of Burgiss's arms and led him away.

It happened so fast that I did not realize until too late that it was done.

"You will all be obligated to be here tomorrow," the official said.

"W-wait," Pelus stammered. "You-you can't choose one of the mentors—"

"As I said, Pelus," the official said coolly, "these were unusual circumstances, and those circumstances justified our unusual choice. His age is still suitable, and this year's class may be the first one where every student has learned to walk in the Light."

"You can't..." Pelus started.

"The mentors can now escort their students back to the retraining area," the official said. "Tomorrow morning, after the morning meal, you will all return here, and after the ceremony, you will all be free to leave."

No one moved. I could hear my pulse counting the time. Until, finally, Pelus was the first person to turn around.

I did not make the decision to move. My legs moved for me. The rest of me was still in shock.

It wasn't until I stepped back into that giant room that it fully sank in what had just happened.

Beside me, Marvus swore.

I glanced, expecting someone to reprimand him. No one did. I looked to Pelus. Pelus stood still as a statue.

"Pelus," I said, "I'm sorry."

Pelus looked at me. The air seemed to tremble around him.

"I was prepared to lose you," Pelus said. "I was not prepared to lose him again."

He turned away. I heard the main door close behind him.

"Kimi," Marvus asked, "are you okay?"

It took me a moment to process that Marvus had spoken to me. "Um, yeah."

"I'm not," Marvus said.

"Yeah," I admitted. "I'm not either."

Did Halmo know? Would he know? I wished I could tell him.

But above all, I wished that I knew where Burgiss was now.

## 14

I expected Braghin and Jaim to be harsher than ever that night. But they weren't. I think maybe they were in as much shock as everyone else. Or maybe I just shut them out. I couldn't really think of anything except Burgiss.

I couldn't sleep. I couldn't eat. How could I do either when I knew what would happen in a few hours?

How was Burgiss bearing this?

I regretted now not telling him what Halmo and I were doing. If only he could at least know what was happening to the Light. Would it provide him a little comfort? A little hope?

Did Halmo know? How close was he to being done? His new Light had come along so fast.

Don't hope for a miracle.

But I couldn't help it. I hoped. And the hope hurt like a dagger.

I could not tell whether the dread of today was heavier than the dread of the day before. It was different, certainly, but I could not tell which one weighed me more.

In the ceremony room, I stood beside Pelus and Marvus. I could hear the others whispering. I was too overwhelmed to process what they said, only to notice the meanness in the undertones of their voices. I was more interested in the back of the room where one of the officials and the shadow-snatcher were talking.

"The door is unlocked?" I heard the official almost whispering.

"It is unlocked," the shadow-snatcher whispered back.

"Is he ready?" the official asked.

"As ready as he ever was," the shadow-snatcher replied.

"You spoke with him?" the official asked.

"As much as I was able," the shadow-snatcher said. "He cursed me all the while, and he was still cursing me after I left. To the very last, he was rejecting the Light. You chose well. This is the only good that can come from such a shadowed soul."

"A sad thing," the official said. "He had a second chance, something most shadowed people never have, and he only seemed to sink deeper into darkness."

"A tragedy," the shadow-snatcher agreed. "Usually, I would be expected to provide comfort to the mentor. I assume this time you want me to be there to support his student."

"If you please," the official said.

I made an effort to hide my distaste as the shadow-snatcher came to me. I tried not to respond to his footsteps or to flinch when the edge of his robe brushed my arm. I tried to ignore his chemical smell.

"I know it's especially hard for you," the shadow-snatcher said.

"It's the way of things," I said flatly.

"Even so," the shadow-snatcher said, "it must be hard."

"It is," I said.

"I know it was hard for you to learn the ways of the Light," the shadow-snatcher said. "You grew up with only shadows. But you have come very far, and you should be proud of yourself."

"Right," I said, jaw-clenched. What I wanted to say was...

In fact, why didn't I say it?

"It was only because of Burgiss," I said.

Fool, I told myself. I'd given him more reason to talk to me now.

"It was not your mentor," the shadow-snatcher said. "It was you. Your mentor erred in his ways again and again, but you found the path to the Light."

My anger was too much. "Will you shut up?"

I heard someone take a breath. I heard the silence.

"Some people process their pain better with quiet," the shadow-snatcher said. His voice seemed to carry to someone else.

Sure, I thought. Let's leave it at that.

One of the officials cleared his throat.

"Every year," the official said, "we take in the few youths who struggle most to find the Light. We watch them grow. We watch them try to learn. And most of them do learn. But every year, with great heartache, we must acknowledge that one person will not."

A door opened. A man came in. Behind him, I almost could not recognize the footsteps. They were so shuffled, so timid, but they were Burgiss's.

Burgiss never came close enough for me to see him well, but I could catch glimpses. I saw the ropes around his wrists, bound in front of him. I saw the way his figure visibly trembled. I caught a snatch of his face. He was so pale that I thought he would faint.

The man pressed on Burgiss's shoulders. I saw Burgiss kneel. I heard his knees thud against the floor. I heard his shaky breaths.

"To our heartbreak," the man said, "this shadowed young man has been one of our greatest failures. Most of our students have only one year to be retrained. This shadowed man had five. Through all of those five years, he remained incurably drawn to darkness. Again and again, he chose darkness over Light, even to his last hours."

I heard Burgiss take in a long breath, releasing it in a wavering sigh.

"The Light sustains us," the man said. "It guides us, provides for us, and shields us from the darkness of the world. But in return, we must give someone of our own so that the Light will not fade. The Light cannot sustain itself on its own. And so, with heavy hearts, we choose one person each year who cannot let the Light into themselves.

"Perhaps we are fortunate. For the price of a single life, a few hundred more survive. Our food grows hearty, our water runs clean, and our lives are healthy and safe. But that does not change the sorrow this sacrifice brings."

I heard a door open. It was not a normal door, though. This was sideways, and it opened upward. An intense brightness came through it, so bright that I flinched. I heard every student gasp. Burgiss shielded his face with his forearms.

I heard the woman and the other man moving toward Burgiss.

"May the Light accept the one we give over," the speaker said.

The others lifted Burgiss, all but throwing him forward. He screamed.

The light grew sharply brighter for a second, and I flinched. My stomach shoved itself sickeningly into my chest.

The door closed.

The Light was already starting to steadily brighten here. The buzzing was a little higher-pitched now.

*I hate to think this Light is all that's left of him.*

I felt my heart suddenly race. I didn't feel myself move. But a moment later, I felt tight arms on me.

"Stop fighting, kid," Pelus's voice came. "It's too late."

I struggled.

"He's gone."

The pain in his voice is what made me stop fighting. He let go.

The thought that any of this light could be Burgiss turned my stomach so much that I gagged. It might not be, I told myself. Maybe Halmo was on time.

"For one more year," the official said, "we will be sustained. You are welcome to leave any time, or to take as much time as you need."

I didn't move. I stared toward the door. All I wanted to do was open it, just to see that my worst thoughts weren't true.

Did Halmo know?

"Kimi," Pelus said, "you know he gave his life to save yours."

"I know," I said, still staring at the door.

"I had to tell Burgiss this once before," Pelus said. I heard his voice choke. "He lost his life to save yours. You must not make it be in vain."

I turned to him. I took his hand, squeezing it.

"I know," I said. "Thank you."

"Kimi," the shadow-snatcher said, "I don't know where you plan to go now."

I still looked at the door. If it was what I thought, though, if there was any hope of it being true, no one else could see.

I looked down. "I want to go home. If I can leave. I'll tell the others not to bother you, and you'll never have to fear us again."

"Kimi," Marvus said, "are you sure?"

Marvus might have been the one person left who could make me think twice. But no. As good a friend as he was, as worried about him as I was, there was no reason to stay.

"Yeah, I'm sure," I said.

Marvus hugged me so tightly that the air was knocked out of me.

"I'm going to miss you, Spy," Marvus said.

"I'll miss you too, bud," I said.

He hugged me tightly, then let go.

"Well, good luck out there," Marvus said. "I'll be thinking of you."

"Yeah, you too," I said.

"I'll escort you home, Marvus," Pelus mumbled.

"Pelus?" I asked. "Are you going to be alright?"

"There is another year of students waiting," Pelus said.

"Wait here a little while, Kimi," the shadow-snatcher said. "I'll speak to the officials to make sure I can escort you out."

Marvus gave me one more hug. I hugged him tightly back. He hesitated a long time before he turned to leave. Pelus lingered a moment longer but said nothing. And then the door closed behind them.

They couldn't know, but I knew. It was not forever.

Suddenly, I felt tight hands on me. I gasped. Those same hands jerked me heavily onto the platform.

"W-what are you doing?!" I exclaimed.

The hands turned me so the shadow-snatcher was staring directly into my eyes. "Do you think I am going to allow you to go back to the darkness? After all you have learned about the Light? If you had accepted the Light into your heart, you would not go back, so you can only be leaving to bring the shadows back to claim us."

"W-what?" I stammered. "No—no—"

I stammered my protests as he pulled me toward the door. I heard it wrench open. The light was blinding.

Bodily, he threw me in. I screamed.

I landed on something soft. I heard a grunt beneath me and hoped my scream had hidden it.

The Light flashed brightly as the door slammed closed.

How loud the buzzing was in here.

I heard a click of a lock. Distantly, I heard the footsteps leave. Only when I no longer heard them did I dare move.

Burgiss was definitely under me. He was still warm, and I still heard his breath.

I brought a hand to his shoulder.

"Burgiss," I whispered, "are you okay?"

Burgiss groaned.

"You're okay now," I eased. "We just have to—"

"I didn't know," Burgiss croaked. "I didn't know that...that we have to wait before the Light..."

"No, Burgiss, it's okay," I eased. "We just have to wait for Halmo to let us out."

Burgiss flinched under my hand, fixing me with a feverish stare. "You mean Halmo is the one who feeds us—"

"No," I interrupted. "Burgiss, we changed the Light. It doesn't need to eat anymore."

Burgiss stared. "Changed...the..."

"Halmo can explain," I said. "You know that day when we were gone all day? We were going to look at—"

I heard footsteps, and then I heard a click. The panel moved with a wooden groan, and Halmo's silhouette appeared.

"Kimi?" Halmo asked. "Burgiss?"

"Yeah, we're both here," I said. "Thanks for covering."

"I didn't think I was going to make the Light flash on time the second time," Halmo said. "Kimi, need a hand?"

I reached out, using Halmo's arm for balance to climb out.

"Burgiss, hold on," Halmo said. "Let me get those ropes off of you."

He reached in, pulling at the binding. I wondered if I could help, but there wasn't room. Halmo made short work of the knots, dropping the rope aside, before reaching back to pull Burgiss out. Burgiss was still trembling, and when he got to his feet, he still leaned on Halmo for support.

"Are you alright?" Halmo asked.

"My leg fell asleep," Burgiss said.

"Here, Burgiss," Halmo said. "Have a seat."

Burgiss sank down. He still looked winded.

"I still don't understand," Burgiss said.

"I'm sorry we couldn't tell you before," Halmo said. "We thought it was going to be Kimi, not you. Kimi and I, we've been working for many months to replace the Light with something that does not need to eat. And up until a week ago, I didn't think I'd be on time. I couldn't tell you before they chose a sacrifice because your reaction had to be genuine to not give it away, but I thought I would have the chance to tell you the night before."

"Did Kimi know?" Burgiss asked.

"Only partially," Halmo said. "The last time I saw him, I told him it was possible but not certain. I still didn't know until late last night that I'd have the Light replaced enough to remove its intake."

"But you did it," I said.

"I did," Halmo said. "I've pulled more all-nighters the last couple of months than I thought I could possibly pull, but I did it."

"What happened?" Burgiss asked. "How did you change the Light?"

"Kimi showed me a few other different sources of light," Halmo explained. "I tried a few combinations over the months and found a fast-growing combination of light-giving insects, algaes, and krella, and over the last two months I have been slowly replacing the Light with this new light-giving biome. It will be a few more months before it grows enough to replace the whole Light, but it will finish growing before the remaining Light runs out of energy."

Burgiss rubbed at his temples. "This is hurting my head."

"Basically," Halmo said, "you know how when we were kids we made terrariums sometimes? I'm doing something similar, but at a large scale, and only with species that give off light."

"So, they don't have to feed anyone to the Light again?" Burgiss asked.

"No, they don't," Halmo said. "But the Light will still need care. It will need more care than ever. It will take the efforts of all three of us, but especially you two because you can always be here. I will need to be in the city, partly because I am expected and partly so we know what is happening in the city."

Burgiss's voice wavered, but I heard that a smile still shaped his tones. "They'd be so happy to know. My students, and...all of them."

"They would," Halmo agreed.

Burgiss looked up at the Light. His head moved as he traced the new Light. When he looked back to Halmo to speak, his voice was still formed around a smile.

"How do we care for the Light?" Burgiss asked.

"I'll teach you," Halmo said. "And every year, it will get a little easier."

"How?" Burgiss asked.

"You know as well as I do that there are people who derive their power from the yearly ceremony. They won't give it up without a fight, and they will be angry if they find out it was taken from them."

"Right," Burgiss said.

"So," Halmo said, "we won't tell them. And every year, we'll have a new person to help us in exchange for keeping them hidden. And the intake, I have time to make it better so we can get them out quickly so they don't give us away mid-ceremony."

"It won't work forever, Halmo," Burgiss said. "One of them is going to betray us."

"Eventually," Halmo said. "By then, we'll have had the new Light for years. There won't be much they can do to bring the old Light back. And we'll play it by ear, see who each new person is. And that's another reason for me to be in the city: so we know in advance who the new helper will be. It might help us to have someone inside the retraining too. Do you still agree that Pelus would be able to keep a secret?"

"He can," Burgiss agreed, sitting up a little straighter.

"Then I'll tell him when I am next able to see him," Halmo said.

"That will make the old man happier than he's been his entire life," Burgiss said.

Halmo hummed his agreement.

"And what do we do when they find us out?" Burgiss asked.

"We have time to figure that out," Halmo said. "By the end of the year, we will know what to do."

—

I know you're shaken to learn this, so many years later. You feel guilty, I know, and confused, perhaps even betrayed. How hard it must be to trust such a frail promise from a stranger when even the firmest old assurance of stability has fallen away. But given time, I promise, it's going to be alright. We'll teach you how to care for your Light now.

*Emma Okell*

## Acknowledgment

Thank you to Kaitlin Lyle for being my test-reader and helping me to find initial errors. Thank you to Arkettype for helping me to edit, format, and publish this book. Thank you to the Youth Climate Collaborative for giving me the encouragement to think my writing was worthy of reading. And thank you to my parents for not letting me give up on publishing my writing.

## About The Author

Emma Okell has been writing since they could hold a pen and invented their first nom de plume when they were four. They previously published two books under the pseudonym Olana Stuart. Their short story "The Cooking Spoon" was recently published in the Youth Climate Collaborative's publication *Climate Courage*. For more information visit **https://www.youthcc.org/store/climate-courage-journals** or **emmaokell.com**.

## About The Cover Artist

Olivia Montoya is a solo hobby developer/designer, zinester, community builder, event organizer, speaker, and graphic designer. They are in their element working on game and game-adjacent projects, especially narrative video games, tabletop role-playing games, and live action role-playing games. You can see their work on **oliviamontoya.com**.

www.ingramcontent.com/pod-product-compliance
Lightning Source LLC
LaVergne TN
LVHW010220070526
838199LV00062B/4669